READY TO POUNCE

The huge cat snarled, a fierce, hissing cry that caused Evelyn King's pony to whinny and shy. Evelyn was so scared, she forgot to firm her grip on the reins. Her mount bounded to the left, brushing against a boulder, and pain seared her leg.

In a lithe leap the mountain lion reached the lip of the high boulder it was on. Crouching to spring, it snarled again, its black-tipped tail twitching.

Evelyn gaped up into savagely piercing eyes, horrible orbs that seemed to stab icy claws deep down inside of her. She knew she should wheel her pony around and get out of there but her limbs would not move.

The painter's whole body went rigid. Her pa had told her mountain lions did that when they were about to attack.

WILDERNESS

#25

FRONTIER MAYHEM

← **David Thompson** →

LEISURE BOOKS NEW YORK CITY

To Judy, Joshua, and Shane.

A LEISURE BOOK®

September 1998

Published by

Dorchester Publishing Co., Inc.
276 Fifth Avenue
New York, NY 10001

ISBN 0-8439-4433-1

FRONTIER MAYHEM

Chapter One

Zebulon Clark was scared. He did not want to die. Given his druthers, he would like to live a long, prosperous life. Often he had imagined himself as an old man, seated in a rocking chair with an adorable grandchild perched on a knee. He wanted to end his days peacefully, to pass on to the other side quietly, in his sleep.

Fate had other ideas.

The first inkling Zebulon had of trouble was when the forest suddenly went quiet. Totally, utterly silent. All the birds stopped chirping. All the squirrels stopped chattering. The chipmunks no longer scampered playfully about. It was as if every living thing had abruptly died. Or was in hiding.

Zebulon had halted and cocked his head to listen. He'd figured it was a roving grizzly or a prowling painter, and he had not been particularly concerned. After all, he had his trusty Hawken and a brace of flintlock pistols. Plus his butcher knife.

Then a shrill whistle had pierced the rarified mountain

7

air. A cry like that of a hawk—only a hawk was not the source. No, an earthbound predator had uttered that cry, and it was answered by another, then a third.

Savages! The word pealed in Zebulon's head like the clap of doom. He'd come to take it for granted the valley was a safe haven, that Indians rarely if ever came there. He should have known better.

For months Zeb had gone blithely on with his work; setting traps, skinning beaver, each day adding to his collection of prime peltries. He'd long since acquired more than the packhorses could carry. The extras would be toted by his mount, and Lou's saddle horse. So what if they had to walk clear back to St. Louis? The inconvenience was worth it.

Lou had suggested they leave while the going was good. But Zebulon always refused. By the grace of God they had stumbled on a beaver paradise, and Zebulon was not about to leave until he had every last hide there was to be had.

Lou had come right out and said he was being a mite greedy. Yes, he was, yet Zebulon couldn't help himself. Not when it would add a couple of hundred dollars to the final tally. An entire year's worth of income for most folks back home.

"Another week," Zebulon kept insisting. "Just one more and we'll go. I promise."

One week had become three.

Now, Zebulon could not help but wonder if his greed might cost them dearly. Turning, he retraced his steps, heading for camp. The traps slung over his shoulder clanked and rattled. Newhouses were costly, but not worth his life. Dropping them, he hurried on, what little noise he made drowned out by a gurgling stream on his left.

The hawk cry was repeated, this time from a thicket on the opposite bank. Nervously fingering the Hawken's trigger, Zebulon picked up the pace. His mouth had gone as dry as a desert; his palms were sweaty.

Please, Zebulon prayed, *please let them hold off until we load up and light a shuck.* It would be folly to try and take the plews. Every precious second wasted was another closer to the grave. Anyone with half a brain would forget the hides and just *ride.* But they had gone to so much trouble. He owed it to Lou, and to his beloved wife. Bless her departed soul.

It was over a mile to the clearing. A harrowing mile, every step possibly his last. Zebulon's buckskins were plastered to his skin and his scalp was prickling as if from a heat rash when at last he spotted the horses and the bales and Lou sharpening a scraper on a whetstone.

Zebulon opened his mouth to shout, but his throat was too dry. All he could do was squeak, like a pathetic tiny mouse.

Lou had not noticed the danger. Which was understandable. The blue sky, the lazy pillowy clouds that drifted overhead, the gentle breeze rustling the slender aspens, all conspired to give a person a false sense of peace and security.

Zebulon had to swallow three or four times before his vocal chords would work. By then he was at the clearing's edge, and swore he could feel unseen eyes bore into his back. "Lou!" he said urgently. His pride and joy swung around, a warm smile nipped in the bud.

"Pa? What's the matter?"

"Trouble," Zebulon said, struggling to stay calm, to keep his tone level. He imagined Lou scalped and staked out naked, and inwardly quaked. *Dear Lord! No!* It was bad enough he had lost Lou's ma to the fever. He wouldn't lose their offspring, too! Not when he had promised Marcy to take special care of the child, to see to it that Lou grew up to be a credit to them both.

"What kind of trouble, Pa?"

Anxiety tore at Zebulon's vitals. Lou was so young, so tender. Only sixteen. Sweetly innocent sixteen. It would be the ultimate injustice to deprive someone that age of life, and future happiness. "Injuns." Zebulon's voice was raspier than he intended thanks to a constriction in his throat.

Lou scanned the woods. "What tribe?"

"I don't rightly know," Zebulon admitted. "They ain't shown themselves yet."

"Maybe they're friendly."

"Not likely. Peaceable Injuns don't skulk about swapping birdcalls. I got a powerful bad feeling about this." Zebulon motioned. "Mount up and head for the pass. I'll be along directly."

"And leave you here alone?"

Raw emotion threatened to wash over Zebulon in a tidal wave of commingled grief and joy. "Don't sass me now, child. It ain't the right time or place."

Lou was moving toward another rifle, propped on a log. "I'm not a sprout anymore. I can do as I darn well please."

"For my sake. Go."

"No."

"Just like your ma," Zebulon said softly, more to himself than to Lou. His darling Marcy had possessed a stubborn streak a mile wide. Otherwise, she had been as fine a wife as any man ever had. Tender, considerate, and playful under the bedcovers.

Another piercing cry reminded him they did not have a moment to spare. He glanced at the peltries, reluctant to part with a single one. Yet some had to be left behind or they would lose their lives. "Saddle Old Jake and Fancy. I'll load the pack animals."

"We're taking an awful risk."

That they were. Sensible trappers would ride off bareback and forget the hides. But Zebulon couldn't, not even when his life depended on it. He ran to the bales and hauled one toward the string.

Lou worked quickly, one eye on the vegetation. Zebulon's obvious fear was more unnerving than the Indians. Somehow or other Lou had gotten the notion that Zebulon was not afraid of anything. To learn differently was deeply unsettling.

Lou's slim fingers fumbled with the cinch. Jaw muscles tightening, Lou concentrated. *Stay calm!* a tiny inner voice said. *Do what has to be done and you'll get out of this with your own skins intact!*

Or would they?

Lou stiffened at the sight of a shadowy figure in the forest. A warrior had stepped from behind a trunk to brazenly watch what they were doing. Murky shadow hid the man's features, but Lou could tell the Indian was painted for war, and that was all that really mattered. "Oh, Lord."

"What?" Zebulon stopped and gazed in the same direction. His blood became ice; his heart skipped a beat. Without thinking, he snapped the Hawken to his shoulder and thumbed back the hammer, but before he could fire the figure disappeared.

Lou was glad. A shot would provoke the war party into attacking. "Forget the plews, Pa. Let's skedaddle. I'll cover you while you saddle Old Jake." Lou moved a few feet to one side, puzzled when Zebulon stood there like a bump on a log. "What are you waiting for, Pa? Hurry!"

"You're asking me to give up two thousand dollars worth of beaver! More money than I've had at one time in all my born days. Money that can give us a decent life back in the States."

"Money ain't worth dying over."

Zebulon did not seem to hear. "I can send you to school, just like your ma always wanted. She made me promise her, you know. On her deathbed. And I aim to stand by my word, come Hell or high water."

"Please, Pa. Just get on Old Jake."

"It galls me, child. Galls me something fierce. We've worked godawful hard for these pelts." Zebulon felt a funk coming on, and didn't care. "Getting up at the crack of dawn every day. Wading in cold water up to my chest.

About freezing my toes off more times than I care to recollect. Lugging those heavy beaver. All the skinning and curing we've done. And for what? For a bunch of mangy red devils to steal it all out from under us and leave us broke?''

"Pa! For God's sake!''

"I refuse!'' Zebulon raged, wagging the Hawken. "Do you hear me, damn your bones! The Clark clan doesn't give up easily! Try to run us off and there will be blood shed! Mark my words!''

An arrow whizzed out of the greenery and imbedded itself in Zebulon's ribs with a loud *thunk*. The impact jolted him backwards and partially spun him around. Amazement etched his face. Then agony spiked through him like a red-hot poker. He buckled at the knees.

"No!'' Lou bounded to Zebulon's side and grabbed him around the shoulders. Specters flitted among the trees, drawing closer. "Pa, we have to get you out of here! Help me! I can't do it alone!''

Zebulon tried to stand, but his legs refused to obey. Weakness overwhelmed him. The world whirled as if caught in the grip of a tornado, and his stomach roiled like butter in a churn. Bile rose in his gorge. "Leave me,'' he gasped.

"Never!'' Frantic, Lou bent, wedged a shoulder under Zeb's arm, and levered upward. The strain was almost more than Lou could bear. Sinews quivering, they staggered toward their mounts.

The specters were closer, a ring of dusky warriors in buckskins, many holding bows, some armed with lances, a few hefting eyedaggs. Foremost was a tall man whose dark eyes danced with vitality. He strode into the open as fearlessly as if entering his own village. Red stripes had been painted on his forehead and cheeks, lending him an especially frightening aspect.

Lou pretended the Indians were not there. Paying them no mind was hard, but the only way to stave off paralyzing fear. "Hold on, Pa. I'll have us out of here in two shakes of a lamb's tail. You can count on me.''

Zebulon barely heard. His head pounded to the pulsing rhythm of his own blood. It was like the time they had visited the ocean and he had stood on a low cliff listening to breakers crash on rocks. Only this was inside him. He could hardly think. ''Lou—'' he began, intending to bid the child to flee.

''Hush. I know what you're going to say and you might as well save your breath. I can no sooner leave you than I can sprout wings and fly.''

The tall warrior stepped between them and the horses. Folding his arms, he regarded them intently, particularly Lou. He acted more amused than anything else, making no attempt to resort to his lance.

Lou was not accustomed to bearing so heavy a burden. Zebulon was a powerful man, weighing upwards 220 pounds. Twice what Lou weighed. Gritting from the exertion, Lou stumbled to a stop. ''Out of my way, varmint.'' When the warrior did not budge, Lou brought the rifle to bear, difficult to do one-handed. ''I mean it! Shoo! Or in another minute you'll be worm food.''

If the warrior understood English, which was highly unlikely, he did not show it. Grunting, he pointed at Zebulon, then at the ground. The meaning was as clear as crystal.

''Go to Hell,'' Lou said, which was as close to a cuss word as Zeb would abide. The click of the hammer being pulled back was unnaturally loud.

A warrior to the south yelled and whipped a bow up, an ash arrow already notched to a taut string. The man sighted down the shaft, squarely at Lou's chest. For a span of five seconds Lou's life hung in the balance. Then the tall warrior gestured, and the bowman reluctantly lowered his weapon.

The odds were twelve to one. Resistance was useless. Yet giving up was never an option. Lou would rather die protecting Zebulon. To surrender would mean torture. Or so many a fellow mountaineer had claimed.

Bracing both legs, Lou trained the rifle on the tall warrior's sternum. "I won't warn you again. Stand aside or else."

Incredibly, the tall man came forward until the muzzle was inches from his wide chest. He even had the audacity to reach out and hold the barrel steady. Other warriors fidgeted uneasily.

Lou was flabbergasted, then recollected being told that Indians valued courage above all else. The tall leader was demonstrating his bravery for all to behold. Virtually daring Lou to shoot.

"Kill him," Zebulon gasped. His senses were still in turmoil, but he had enough presence of mind to realize that if they did not shoot their way out, they were goners. Befuddled when Lou did not obey, he said, "What are you waiting for? Do it, then run like a scalded dog. Don't fret about me. I'll be right behind you." The last was an out-and-out lie. He could not take two steps, let alone run two feet.

Lou's eyes were locked on the tall warrior's. It was a proverbial moment of truth, a crucial turning point. Lou's finger closed on the trigger—but not firmly enough to fire. For Lou had never taken a life before, never so much as raised a fist in anger. Over and over in Lou's mind resounded the Commandment. *Thou shalt not kill!*

"Shoot!"

Lou wanted to. With every fibre, every particle, every iota of being. But the finger on the trigger did not curl any further. Lou saw a smile spread across the Indian's face, and the warrior leaned forward. "I'm sorry, Pa. We're done for."

It was impossible for Zeb to be mad. People had to be true to their nature, and that was all Lou was doing. "We won't let them do us in without a tussle," Zeb vowed, girding himself to rise. They would die, but they would take some of their enemies with them.

Lou let down the hammer and lowered the rifle. There was no use in pretending; the warrior could tell it was a bluff. Regret overwhelmed rising despair. "I've failed you, Pa. Ma must be rolling over in her grave."

"Nonsense." Zebulon's abdomen and upper thighs were slick with warm blood. He was not long for this world. Unless he acted soon, it would be too late.

The tall warrior's bronzed hand rose toward Lou's pale throat, then stopped. Furrows creased the man's brow. His eyes narrowed and he tilted his head. He looked Lou up and down as if amazed. Without warning, he pressed a hand against Lou's chest. Startled, he stepped back and announced his discovery in his own tongue.

"May the Lord preserve us," Zebulon breathed. "They know. Run, girl! Run!"

"No. Clarks have grit. Isn't that what you've taught me since I was knee high to a calf? I'm not leaving you and that's final."

Panic mounted in Zeb. "Louisa May, I'm ordering you to get the hell out of here! Now! Before they force themselves on you!"

"Ma would have a fit if she heard you cuss, Pa."

Zebulon would have added a string of oaths if he'd had the energy. *Only a female would give a hoot about proper behavior when they were both about to be slit from ear to ear!* "Leave me and go, child! Don't let me pass on to my reward with your own death on my conscience. Please."

Lou held her ground. The truth was out. So be it. Ordinarily, her baggy buckskins and short hair were enough to disguise her gender, but the tall warrior had the eyes of a hawk. She placed a hand on her butcher knife. While she could not kill in cold blood, she would do whatever was necessary to keep from being violated. As her ma had always said, there were fates *worse* than death.

The tall leader was talking to several others. An argument broke out, with much motioning and loud words. At the conclusion, the tall man stepped aside and indicated Old Jake and Fancy.

"He's saying we can leave!" Lou exclaimed.

"Not without the plews," Zebulon said. "Make them savvy. We can't go without our hides." An urge to cough doubled him over. Automatically, he raised a hand to cover his mouth. When the fit subsided and he lowered his palm, it was bright scarlet.

Lou did not waste another moment. Setting the rifle down, she wrapped both arms around her father and practically dragged him to the horses. He objected, but he was in no condition to resist. Once next to Old Jake, she had a greater problem: how to get her pa up into the saddle. Unaided, she could never do it.

The tall warrior was examining her rifle. Lou grinned to herself, pointed at the gun, then at the leader. "Like that, do you? It's yours if you'll lend me a hand." She tapped the saddle, then her father's shoulder. "Give my pa a boost."

Clearly perplexed, the warrior did not budge.

"My rifle for helping me," Lou stressed, repeating the pantomime. A gleam of comprehension lit the leader, and he laughed as if it were a joke. But he helped. He came over and without half trying flung Zebulon over the saddle like he would fling a sack of potatoes.

"I'm obliged," Lou said. She was going to climb on Fancy, but a stocky, scarred warrior seized the dun's bridle and spoke angrily. Another heated dispute resulted in the stocky warrior letting go, but he was not happy about it. Sullen as a riled bear, he glared as Lou hooked a foot in a stirrup and swung lithely astride her animal.

She lingered a fleeting second, sadly contemplating the hides that had meant a new life for her pa and her. Those pelts would have insured that she would attend a fine Eastern school. Now her long-nurtured hope of becoming a genuine lady was shattered. Without those peltries, there would be no fine home or lavish carriage or expensive dresses and bonnets. Her special dream would never come to pass.

None of the Indians tried to stop them from leaving. Most of the warriors were busy rummaging through supplies or admiring plews. One man had found the sugar tin, and was dipping a finger in and licking it.

Seizing Old Jake's reins, Lou jabbed her heels against Fancy and broke into a trot. She anticipated an arrow between the shoulder blades, but the Indians were content with their plunder. Why they had spared her, she had no idea. Maybe the leader had taken pity on her. Or maybe they did not believe it fitting to make war on a woman.

A woman? Louisa nearly laughed aloud. Who was she trying to fool? She was only sixteen. A girl, by any standard. But a girl who had done things no other girl her age ever had. Such as traveling far from Virginia, to the remote, majestic Rockies. Such as living in the wild vastness of the high peaks for over a year. Such as surviving encounters with silvertips, to say nothing of summer drought and fall floods and snowstorms that buried whole mountains.

Her mother would have been proud, Lou liked to think. Marcy Bonham Clark had been an independent spirit who did as she darn well pleased, the opinion of others be hanged. She'd married Zeb against the wishes of her parents. She'd lived in the deep woods instead of the city, to the dismay of all her kin. And she had encouraged her husband's hankering to live as a free trapper, despite the hardships. More the pity that Marcy had died before Zebulon headed west.

Or was it a blessing in disguise? Lou wondered. For had her mother been at the camp when the war party struck, she would surely have resisted. And been part of the bloodbath.

A groan reminded Lou of her uppermost responsibility. She dared not slacken the pace, though. Not yet. "Hang on, Pa. As soon as we're out of danger, I'll treat that wound. You'll be all right. Wait and see." He *had* to be all right. Without her father, Lou had a snowball's chance in July of staying alive long enough to reach St. Louis.

Zebulon could not answer. Light-headed, nauseous, disoriented, he shut his eyelids tight and prayed for the awful sensations to go away. The pain, surprisingly, was much less. He took that as a good sign, as an omen he was not severely hurt. He *had* to live, for his daughter's sake.

On through the verdant woodland they hurried, Louisa angling toward the pass that linked their pristine valley to the outside world. Small wonder beaver had been abundant. It was doubtful other whites had ever set foot there.

She thought fondly of the many months spent in their sanctuary. The work had been grueling, what with having to scrape and prepare hide after hide. But the evenings had been delightful. Snugly nestled an arm's length from the crackling flames, she had coaxed her father into talking about her mother, about their courting days, about anything and everything that had to do with their life together. And in the process she had grown closer to him than she had ever been.

On through the pines Louisa went. They covered half a mile, and although her intuition warned they were not yet safe, she reined up and slid down. "Pa," she said tenderly as she carefully eased Zeb off the saddle and gently lowered him onto his back. Shock gave way to horror. His buckskins were drenched, his face as pale as a sheet of paper. "Oh, Pa."

Zebulon heard, and drifted up through a clinging fog into the rosy light of day. "Lou?" Her visage seemed to float above him like a disembodied ghost. "I could use some water, girl. And a blanket. I'm so cold. Why did the temperature drop?"

Louisa noted the beads of perspiration on her father's forehead. How could he be cold and burning up at the same time? The stream was a couple of hundred yards to the north, and the only blankets they had were their saddle blankets. "I'll do what I can. In the meantime, you lie here and don't utter a peep." She started to stand, but his fingers clamped onto her wrist.

"Stay with me."

18

"But you just—."

"I know what I said," Zebulon said, cutting her off. The cold inside of him was expanding at an alarming rate. He was no fool. He knew what it meant. Mustering his waning strength, he went on. "I don't have much time. You must listen."

"Don't talk like this. You're going to be fine. I'll get the arrow out and have you on the mend in—."

Again Zebulon interrupted. "Hush! This is important. Do you remember the Rendezvous we went to last July?"

"Of course. Up to Green River. Not many traders came, and that white-haired man who liked to quote Shakespeare told us it might be the last."

"Do you remember that other nice fella we met? The big man? The one who won the wrestling contest?"

How could Lou forget? He was the only man who had ever beaten her father. And every other trapper, to boot. "Nate King. What about him?"

"I hear tell the Kings live in the vicinity of Long's Peak. They have an honest-to-goodness cabin. Find them. They'll help see you safely to the States."

The full import of what her father was imparting made Louisa feel faint. She had to put both hands flat on the ground for support. "Now you hush. I won't listen to this silliness. Let's dig that arrow out and I'll get a fire started." She gripped the hilt of her knife.

Zebulon Clark stiffened. An ominous black fog was eclipsing the sun and the sky, and his daughter. "Please, no." Zeb moved his lips, trying to form the words, "I love you." But the only sound that escaped his throat was a pitiable whine. Then the swirling fog swallowed him whole and he pitched into an inky abyss.

Louisa May Clark trembled, fighting back tears. Her father was gone! She was alone in the heart of the wilderness! Alone, with only her pistols and her possibles bag!

Heaven help her.

Chapter Two

He was eager to kill and get it over with.

Zachary King had been in the saddle since dawn. It was now the middle of the afternoon, and he was impatient to conclude the hunt. From a shelf thousands of feet up a mountain he gazed out over a magnificent vista. Jagged peaks thrust skyward like spears, many crowned with glistening white mantles. A sea of trees, mostly pine, covered lower slopes in rolling waves. In the distance a bald eagle soared on outstretched wings.

Regal Nature, in all her stirring beauty. The sort of scene that would awe a city dweller. But not young Zach. He had lived in the wilderness all his life. The Rockies were his home. Mammoth earthen giants that reared miles above sea level did not impress him.

Zach glanced down at the tracks he had been following. The bull elk, although stricken, showed no sign of flagging. Occasionally, drops of blood confirmed that Zach's shot had indeed scored.

"Just my luck the bull moved when I fired," Zach

mused aloud, and was immediately upset. Talking to one-self was a white trait. His father did it now and then. Uncle Shakespeare did it all the time. And while he loved them both dearly, he did not care to imitate them. He did not care to act as whites did.

It was a recent development, this dislike of his father's people. Zach knew it upset his parents, but it couldn't be helped. Years of abuse at the hands of complete strangers had left him bitter, resentful.

Zach had the supreme misfortune to be born half white, half Indian. Or, as most whites preferred to brand him, a *breed*. And the majority of whites did not like breeds. They looked down their noses at him and his kind. All because of an accident of birth over which he had no control. It was grossly unfair.

When he was younger Zach had not been bothered by the bigotry. Largely because he had not noticed. Quite naturally, he'd spent most of his time doing what children everywhere did, playing and getting into mischief. It was not until his early teens that he began to realize how widespread the hatred was.

His awakening, as Zach liked to call it, had taken place at a Rendezvous three years before. His father and Shake-speare had been swapping tall tales with other free trap-pers. His mother had been visiting Shoshone kin. So he had ambled off alone, roaming the encampment. While threading among the booths set up by the traders from St. Louis, he had been suddenly seized and thrown roughly to the ground.

"Damn you, breed! Where's the knife you stole?"

Bewildered, Zach had gawked up at a skinny man in homespun clothes who shook a fist in his face. Before he could reply, the man had hauled off and kicked him, hard. Anger had spurred Zach into declaring, "I don't know what you're talking about, mister. I never steal."

"You lyin' breed! The knife was on the counter a few seconds ago. Now it's gone! And you're the only one who was nearby."

Stooping, the man had grasped Zach by the front of his hunting shirt and violently jerked him erect.

"I want my knife, breed. Or so help me, I'll tar you within an inch of your life."

"Let me go!" Zach had protested. He'd pried at the trader's fingers, but he'd been no match for a grown man.

"Where is it?" Enraged, the trader had shaken him as a panther might shake a fawn, shaken him until his teeth crunched together and his bones were fit to break. "Fess up, breed!"

A crowd had gathered. Zach had wished his father were there to teach the brute a lesson. But Nate had been clear across camp, unaware of what was happening. Zach had been on his own.

Since brawn would not help, Zach had tried to reason with his assailant. Hadn't his Uncle Shakespeare always claimed that most disputes could be talked out if everyone involved gave it half a chance? "Calm down, mister. I can prove I didn't take your knife. Just search me. Go ahead."

The man had patted Zach's buckskins, then grunted. "Where'd you hide it, boy?"

"I didn't take it, darn you!"

"Don't sass me, breed."

It was then that the trader had drawn back a calloused hand and slapped Zach across the face. Furious, Zach had punched at the man's arms, kicked at the man's leg, but his blows had had scant effect, earning him another slap, which had set his ears to ringing and his vision to swimming. Dimly, he'd heard someone intervene.

"Let the boy go, Evans."

The trader had snorted. "Leave us alone, Kendall. This isn't your affair."

"I'm making it mine. That boy's father is a close friend. Put him down. Now."

Zach's head had cleared. Blood was trickling from his mouth and his lower lip was split. He beheld his savior clearly; Scott Kendall, a stocky, muscular, flame-haired frontiersman who had visited their cabin many times. The spectators were looking from Kendall to Evans and back again in keen anticipation.

The trader hesitated. His grip slackened, but not all the way. "I tell you this damn breed stole from me. Either he returns what he took or I take it out of his hide."

Scott Kendall casually rested a hand on the smooth butt of a pistol tucked under his wide leather belt. "I won't ask you again."

The threat caused Evans to drop Zach as if he were a hot coal. "Now see here! You have no right to interfere! What's this world comin' to when an honest businessman can't stop a scruffy breed thief from makin' off with valuable merchandise!"

"Honest?" Kendall said, and several of the men in the crowd snickered. "I suppose you are. You've never cheated anyone outright. Unless you count marking up your trade goods three hundred percent just to rob us of every hard-earned penny."

"I have a right to make a profit!"

"An honorable profit, yes." Kendall strolled to the booth, studied the items arranged on the counter, then moved around the far end and scrutinized the grass.

"See here," Evans said. "No one is allowed back there except me and my helper."

Kendall doubled over, and when he straightened he held a folding knife in his right palm. "Is this what you claim the boy took?"

"My word! Where was it?"

"On the ground. Where it landed when you probably bumped it off." Kendall came back around. "You owe Zach King an apology."

"King?" Evans had gulped like a fish out of water. "Did you say King?"

"Didn't you know? Zach is Nate King's boy. You must know Nate. Everyone does." Kendall leaned on the counter. "Don't you recall the time Farley Grant trifled with Nate's wife, Winona? Farley was drunk, sure, but

23

that's no excuse for forcing himself on a married woman. Remember what Nate did when he found out?''

The trader coughed.

"No? Well, I sure do. I was there. Nate walked right up to Farley and hit him in the mouth. Never threatened. Or blustered. Just punched him. Once. Broke Farley's jaw and seven teeth besides.'' Scott Kendall sighed. "It wasn't Farley's lucky year. About the time his mouth healed, the Blackfeet got ahold of him. Fed him to their dogs, the story goes. In bits and pieces.''

Evans fidgeted. "As God is my witness, I didn't know the boy is Nate's son.''

Kendall was thoughtfully rubbing his beard. "Can you imagine how strong a person has to be to bust a jaw with one punch?''

"I don't want any hard feelings.''

"Oh?'' Scott Kendall nodded at Zach. "Then I suggest you start to make amends by apologizing to the one you wronged.''

"Sorry, boy.''

Zach nodded, mad but pacified. His father's friend, to his surprise, was far from satisfied.

"You call that an apology? Really, Evans. Put some feeling into it.'' Kendall snapped his fingers as if at an inspiration. "I have it! Why don't you get down on your knees and beg forgiveness?''

"I'll do no such thing!''

Kendall shrugged. "Suit yourself. Come on, Zach. Let's go find your father. I can't wait to see the look on his face when you report what happened.''

To Zach's astonishment, the trader dropped onto his knees, clasped both hands together, and said, "I'm sorry, boy. Honestly and truly! Sometimes I let my temper get the better of me. Forgive me, will you?''

No one laughed. Everyone, in fact, focused on Zach, awaiting his reaction. It rankled him, but he forced out, "I forgive you, mister. Mistakes happen, I reckon.''

Evans grabbed Zach's hand and pumped vigorously.

"Thank you, boy! Thank you! Tell you what. To further make amends, you're entitled to anything in my booth at five percent off. How'd that be?"

Scott Kendall bellowed like a lanced buffalo. "You call that making amends? Damn, man. You just never give up, do you?" Smirking, he dangled the folding knife between a thumb and forefinger. "If you're in earnest, why not let Zach have this as a token of your repentance?"

"You mean—give it to him?"

"I do."

"For *free*?"

Zach did not understand why so many onlookers erupted in mirth, or why Kendall's expression resembled that of a lynx about to pounce on prey.

"Were you born a skinflint, Evans? Or have you had to work at it over the years?" The brawny trapper flipped the knife straight up into the air, then idly caught it. "Yes, for free. And if you keep raising a fuss, maybe you should throw in an ax and some blankets."

"No, no, no. The knife will do." Evans jumped to his feet, snatched the knife, and shoved it into Zach's palm. "Take it, boy. We're even now, hear? There's no need to go bawlin' to your pa that I mistreated you, eh? We'll let bygones be bygones."

The incident ended. The crowd dispersed. Scott Kendall escorted Zach back to camp and stuck around until Nate and Shakespeare returned. Zach never mentioned the occurrence to his pa, but he later learned Kendall did, and that his father paid the trader a visit late that very night. It was the last year Evans attended the Rendezvous.

As for Zach, the memory of that day burned in his brain ever after, festering like a rank sore. He could not forget how unjust the man had been. Nor how many times Evans had referred to him, in contempt, as a "breed."

It was a revelation.

Zach got to thinking back. He recollected many instances when white men had treated him with barely concealed dislike. Concealed, no doubt, because they feared the wrath of his father. And other times when whites had called him a breed to his face, but did so wearing false smiles. As if that would lessen the hurt.

Deeply troubled, Zach had gone to Shakespeare McNair. He often found it easier to talk to Shakespeare than to his parents. McNair always listened without criticizing. That night the white-maned mountaineer had explained the "wicked ways of the world," to use McNair's own words.

"It's always the same old story, Zachary. Since the days of Cain and Abel, folks have hated each other for hate's sake. They hate what they don't understand. They hate whatever they fear. They hate anyone who is different. There are whites who hate Indians for being Indian, and Indians who hate whites for being white."

"And they hate breeds, too," Zach had said.

Sorrow had gripped the old mountain man, and he had tenderly placed a hand on Zach's shoulder. "Children of mixed heritage suffer the worst of both worlds. Whites despise them because they're part Indian, and Indians distrust them because they're part white. I'm afraid you're in for a rough haul, son. Slings and arrows and the like."

"What?"

Shakespeare had done what Shakespeare loved to do. He'd quoted his namesake. " 'To be or not to be, that is the question. Whether 'tis nobler in the mind to suffer the slings and arrows of outrageous fortune, or to take arms against a sea of troubles, and by opposing end them.' " McNair had squeezed him. "Do you understand?"

Zach had nodded. Usually when Shakespeare quoted the Bard, Zach had no inkling whatsoever of what the quote meant. This time he did. It meant people would dislike him even when he did nothing to deserve it. They would despise him simply for *being* himself.

26

From that day on, Zach associated less and less with his father's kind. His eyes opened. He learned that many he had formerly regarded as friends in fact only tolerated him because they liked his father. And many who had always welcomed him with smiles in fact could not abide his guts.

They did not come right out and say so. They did not have to. Zach read the truth in fleeting glances, in subtle expressions. He grew to sense when others loathed him, and he avoided them ever after.

It was not quite as bad among his mother's people. By and large the Shoshones were more tolerant of his mixed blood, but not as tolerant as he would have liked. Quite a few warriors made no secret of their loathing.

To be fair, not all whites were bigots. Decent men like Scott Kendall accepted him and treated him no differently than they treated everyone else. Zach was grateful, but it did not change his outlook.

He had made an important decision. In order to live happily, he must avoid whites except when absolutely necessary.

Zach never explained his decision to his folks. He doubted they would understand. Or if they did, they wouldn't approve. On numerous occasions one or the other had commented that he was becoming too much of a loner. That he should have more dealings with people.

If his father and mother only knew!

Zach shook his head to clear the cobwebs and prodded the sorrel into a brisk walk. It was no use feeling sorry for himself. Warriors were not whiners. As his pa had impressed upon him again and again, "A man must learn to stand on his own two feet. Don't be one of those puny coons who never grow up. Only spoiled weaklings moan and groan when things don't go their way."

The elk's tracks led down a steep incline into thick firs. A deadfall had to be skirted. Beyond, the trail meandered at random, as if the elk were confused. Pools of blood were evidence the bull was on its last legs.

Zach would be glad to butcher it and head home. He had been gone five days, more than he'd intended. But game was hard to find close to the cabin. On every hunt he had to range farther and farther afield.

The pack animals were flagging. In his eagerness to overtake his quarry, Zach had not stopped to rest all day, not even to permit them to drink. A gleaming blue ribbon to the northwest tempted him, but he continued due west for the time being.

The elk had climbed a ridge. Zach prodded the sorrel upward, tugging on the lead rope. He was two thirds of the way to the top when the sorrel snorted and shied. "Steady, fella, steady," Zach said soothingly, then rose in the stirrups. A brownish bulk lay amid scattered boulders.

Zach dismounted and slowly moved higher, his heavy Hawken pressed to his shoulder. Elk were not aggressive by nature, but any cornered creature could be dangerous.

A trapper by the name of Bascomb had found that out the hard way when he'd shot a ten-point black-tailed buck and gone to skin the critter without verifying it was dead. The deer's antlers had sliced his throat wide open. If not for a couple of friends, Bascomb would surely have died.

Yet another reminder that in the wilderness a man could not afford to be careless. One mistake was all it took. One measly mistake might result in an "untimely demise," as Shakespeare called it.

So Zach neared the elk with his rifle cocked and ready. Not much blood surrounded the body, but the bull had already lost a lot. Zach circled to the right to better view the animal's head. The eyes were wide and glazing, the tongue jutted from foam-flecked lips.

"Finally," Zach said, and wanted to kick his own backside for talking to himself again.

Lowering the Hawken, Zach let down the hammer. On the verge of drawing his butcher knife, he turned into the breeze when a faint acrid odor tingled his nostrils. It was smoke. And where there was smoke, there were men.

Quickly, Zach ran to the crest. On the summit he hunkered to avoid silhouetting himself against the sky, as his father had taught him. Crabbing to the west rim, he scoured the rugged terrain below. Isolated mountains were separated by a maze of valleys, ravines, and canyons. Perhaps a quarter of a mile off, gray tendrils wafted above a stand of pines.

"Idiots," Zach said. It had to be whites. Indians would not make camp so early, or reveal their whereabouts so openly. So stupidly.

Zach shrugged and started to turn back. It was no business of his. Whoever they were—trappers, most likely—they meant nothing to him. So what if they were making a blunder that could get them killed? It was their mistake, not his.

Then he paused, thinking of how Scott Kendall had helped him at the Rendezvous. And of times when other whites had treated him kindly. What was it Shakespeare was fond of saying? "We are our brothers' keeper. Whether we want to be or not."

Maybe it wouldn't hurt to take a gander at the yacks, Zach reflected. Just out of curiosity, of course. Few whites ever penetrated so deeply into the mountains. Either these were uncommonly brave—or uncommonly dumb.

After tying the horses to convenient limbs, Zach set forth on foot. A quarter of a mile was nothing to someone who daily hiked ten or more. Plenty of brush provided ample cover. On cat's feet he crept into the stand, flattening when he spied a glimmer of red and orange. He crawled the rest of the way.

A fire burned at the center of a small clearing. Two horses were tethered where they could graze to their heart's content. Two saddles and two saddle blankets had been draped over a log. *So there must be two whites,* Zach deduced, but neither was present.

Typical. The fools had gone off after something for

their supper pot, leaving their animals unprotected. Any wandering Blackfoot or Piegan could help himself. It would serve them right if their horses were stolen and they were stranded afoot.

Zach rested his chin on a forearm. He should leave. Just go on about his business and leave the whites to their own affairs. But part of him, a very small part, bid him stay and see what the pair were up to.

Time dragged by. Zach was restless, anxious to tend to the elk and light a shuck for the cabin. The scent of blood might lure a cougar, or worse, a grizzly, and his horses were as unprotected as those of the whites.

A yellow butterfly flitted across the glade. Sparrows frolicked in a bush. A raven flew overhead, the rhythmic beat of its wings uncommonly loud.

Zach was about at the end of his patience when a figure appeared. A slender figure in very baggy buckskins, a stripling whose close-cropped hair and smooth cheeks marked him as being about the same age as Zach. Over the youth's shoulder was slung a rabbit.

Of the second white, there was no sign. Zach stayed put, content to merely observe. The white youth knelt beside the fire and commenced to skin his catch.

Right away, Zach noticed something peculiar. The youth was in the grip of obvious sadness. Downcast, glum, he worked at a turtle's pace. As empty of zest for life as an upended keg was empty of ale. Zach did not know what to make of it.

Eventually the rabbit had been carved up, and dripping chunks were roasting on a makeshift spit. The youth sat with slim arms wrapped around bent legs, wearing melancholy like a shroud, staring blankly into the depths of the dancing flames.

Zach checked on the sun. In another three hours it would be gone. He must be done with the elk by then. Scavengers would be abroad at the advent of twilight, and he had no yearning to contest possession with a pack of hungry wolves or a ravenous silvertip. Still, he could not tear himself from the youth. Why was the white so upset? Where was the other one? What were they doing so far from the usual trapping haunts?

At length, Zach concluded enough was enough. Either he should show himself or he should leave. And since he would rather shun whites than suffer their spite, he slid backward.

Just then, the youth lowered his face to a sleeve and began to quietly weep.

Stupefied, Zachary stopped. He'd seldom seen a white person cry. Years ago his father had informed him that they considered tears a sign of weakness. That it was against their custom for men to weep openly. Whites were expected to hold their sorrow in, to vent it only when alone. A silly concept.

The Shoshones took the opposite view. They made public displays of their grief. When a loved one died, the women wailed and gnashed their teeth. Those who were blood relatives frequently chopped off part of a finger as a token of their misery. The men took part in a formal ceremony, some slashing themselves with knives, and if tears were shed no one thought poorly of the party who shed them.

Two extremes. And who was to say which was right? Zach certainly was in no position to judge. To his way of thinking, both sides could learn a lot from each other.

The youth was sobbing now, great, racking sobs, as if pent-up torment had found delayed release. His whole body shook as he bent low to the ground, the beaver hat he wore perilously close to the fire.

A strange urge to go comfort the white brought Zach to his knees, but no higher. He was being childish. It would be wrong of him to intrude on the other's woe. He would go butcher the bull and return later.

A twig cracked as Zach padded off, but he thought nothing of it. The youth would not hear. He jogged to the ridge, swinging wide to come up on the site from the north. A precaution, in case unwanted visitors were abroad. But the sorrel and the pack animals were dozing, the bull undisturbed.

Carving up an elk, or any large animals, was not for the squeamish. First, Zach slit the hind legs down the backs of each, cutting entirely around the tail. Next he opened the pelt in a straight line from the chin to the tail, along the belly. The front legs had to be cut, too, starting at the knee joints and ranging to the stomach. Only then was the hide ready to be slowly peeled off, like a glove from a hand. Ligaments and muscle had to be sliced, always keeping the sharp edge of the blade away from the pelt so as not to damage it.

The Shoshones, and most other tribes, did not think highly of elk hides. The pelts did not endure rough use or the elements very well, and were widely rated as inferior to those of deer and antelope. Which was why nearly all the buckskins worn by Indians were fashioned from the former.

Winona, though, never allowed any part of an animal go to waste. She used elk hides mainly for robes worn only indoors. All four members of the family owned one, but Zach rarely used his. It was unseemly. A true warrior did not let a trifling morning chill effect him.

Shakepeare McNair, however, owned a robe Zach would not mind wearing. The fur was solid white and luxuriously thick. McNair had traded a Piegan for it decades ago, back when Piegans were still friendly to whites. The Piegan, in turn, had obtained it from a member of a tribe rumored to live near the top of the world. No one knew what kind of animal it came from. Shakespeare claimed a bear, but everyone scoffed. White bears? It was preposterous.

Zach shifted position to slice into the abdomen. He had to dig out the innards. Then he would treat himself to the heart, raw. The first time his father had offered him one, he had about gagged. Now he could bite into any blood-drenched organ without a second thought. Inserting the blade, he grasped the hilt with both hands.

32

There was a metallic click to his rear, the unmistakable sound of a gun hammer being cocked.

''Don't move! Don't so much as twitch—or you're dead!''

Chapter Three

Zachary King was fit to be tied. He prided himself on
his woodcraft, on being able to sneak up on anyone, anywhere, anytime. It was unthinkable that someone should
do the same to him. He was a Shoshone warrior, or
would be soon enough, and warriors did not let themselves be taken by surprise. His mind racing, he started
to ease the butcher knife from the elk's belly, but froze
when the hard muzzle of a gun was jammed against the
back of his head.

"I said don't move!" warned the one who had jumped
him. "I doubt you savvy English, you mangy Indian, but
this ought to make my meaning plain."

Anger flared in Zach's chest, but he held it in check.
It was easy to mistake him for a Shoshone, what with
the beaded buckskins his mother had made him and the
style in which he wore his long black hair. But *mangy*?

"If you can understand me, raise your hands. And no
tricks."

Should he or shouldn't he? Zach wondered. There

could be an advantage to playing dumb. It might be easier to catch his captor off guard. So he didn't move.

"I guess you don't speak my lingo, huh? Figures."

Out of the corner of an eye Zach saw the youth sidle around to the left. A pistol was trained on Zach's temple, and knowing how jumpy whites could be, he did not so much as lift a finger. Up close, he could see the youth was haggard and grimy. Blue eyes studied him intently.

Louisa May Clark would never admit as much, but she was struck by how handsome the Indian was. Neatly braided hair and broad shoulders added to the allure. She chided herself for admiring him when by rights she should shoot him dead. Indians had killed her pa, hadn't they? But this one was different; his hair and buckskins were not the same as those who were responsible. He might well be from a friendly tribe, for all she knew. "Take your hands off that pigsticker." She motioned to accent her demand.

Zach complied.

"Hands in the air," Lou said, lifting her left arm to demonstrate.

Doing as he was told, Zach coiled his leg muscles, hoping the youth would step just a little bit closer.

"Now move back." Lou pumped her hand, and when the Indian had done so, she yanked the knife out of the elk and tossed it into some weeds.

Zach almost lit into the cuss then and there. Knives did not come cheap. That one was a prized gift from a Shoshone uncle, Touch the Clouds, who had bestowed it on him on his last visit to his mother's people.

Lou gnawed on her lower lip. What was she to do? Earlier she'd heard a twig snap and glimpsed him fading into the undergrowth. Suspecting he was part of a war party and had gone to fetch the rest, she had given chase. But all he'd seemed interested in was the elk. Odd, she mused, that he had spied on her and not tried to harm her. Maybe he really was friendly. "What tribe are you from?" she asked, even though it was pointless.

Zach branded the youth a greenhorn. Most any white who had been in the mountains for any length of time would be able to tell. He noticed dark bags under the youth's eyes, and how extraordinarily slender the youth's hands were.

Fatigue clouded Lou's mind. Four days had gone by since her pa was slain, and she had hardly slept a wink in all that time. Today, she'd made camp much sooner than was her custom for the express purpose of finally catching up on her sleep, but now she had a young savage on her hands. How young, exactly? She figured he couldn't be much older than she was, and that was encouraging. An adult would be more difficult to manage.

Being stared at annoyed Zach. He wished the youth would say or do something to give him some clue as to what was in store. That he had not already been shot dead was a good sign. He would just like to be permitted to go on with the carving. The white boy could jump off a cliff, for all he cared.

Louisa wagged her pistol. "Move to the horses," she directed, nodding. When the Indian did not obey, she assumed he did not comprehend. To make it plainer, she whinnied.

It took all of Zach's self-control not to bust out laughing. Any Shoshone five-year-old could whinny better than that! Imitating animal calls and sounds was a favorite childhood pastime.

"The horses!" Lou said, stamping a foot in frustration.

Zach was not pleased at how the pistol jiggled. The slightest accidental pressure, and the flintlock might discharge. At that range it would blow a hole in him the size of a melon. To calm his captor down, he backed away, halting when he reached the sorrel.

Louisa was delighted she had gotten her point across. Sidestepping to the pack animals, she helped herself to a coil of rope. More like rawhide cord, it suited her purpose perfectly. "I want you to kneel and put your arms behind your back," she instructed, sinking onto her own knees as an example.

Zach would have leaped if not for the pistol. It galled him to be bound. His little charade had gone far enough. He would confess who he was and she would see he was no threat, then go her merry way. He cleared his throat.

As edgy as a mouse in a barn full of cats, Lou jumped up. "Don't you try anything, damn you," she growled. "I'd as soon kill you, you rotten red bastard. Every last one of your kind should be exterminated." It was her grief talking, not her heart. Her misery at her loss caused her to express sentiments she did not believe.

Bigotry again. Zach clenched his fists in outrage. This youth was no different from the vast majority of whites, who liked to say that the only good Indian was a dead one. No less a personage than President Andrew Jackson had pushed for the removal of every last red man from all land the whites coveted, by any means deemed necessary.

"Do it!" Lou ordered.

Zach would rather eat glass. He could still avoid being bound, but he was not about to grovel. Not after that last comment. Scornfully, he knelt and thrust his arms out.

Louisa could see the Indian was mad. She couldn't blame him. But her own safety came before all else. She looped the rope around his wrists enough times to insure he'd never break free, then tied a knot one-handed. Only when she was confident he couldn't harm her did she put down the flintlock to finish the job and cut the extra rope off.

"There. That should hold you."

Zach was as angry at himself for not resisting as he was at the white youth for binding him. The first chance he got, he was going to give the upstart a walloping he would never forget.

Lou walked to the elk. An hour earlier she had beaned a small rabbit with a rock, rather than shoot it and risk having the shot heard. It was only her second meal since the tragedy. But elk meat was tastier. She helped herself, slicing off a chunk large enough to feed five.

Zach grew madder by the second. Stealing someone else's food was about as low as a person could sink. It was not quite as rotten as stealing a horse, but he wouldn't put it past the youth to do that before they were done.

Cradling the bloody meat under her left arm, Lou pointed her flintlock. "All right. I'm taking you back with me. No funny business, you red heathen."

It was too stupid for words, Zach reflected. The fool kept on talking to him even though he supposedly did not understand a lick of English. In Shoshone, he responded, "You are the dumbest white boy I have ever met. Your mother was an ox, your father a lizard. When I get loose, I am going to beat you within an inch of your life."

Louisa smiled. "Well, that's a start. At least you're trying to communicate."

Zach sighed.

"You'll have to bear with me," Lou told him. "It's nothing personal. But your kind are as treacherous as rattlers."

Your kind. The supreme insult. Zach bristled and replied coldly in Shoshone, "Were you dropped on your head as a child? You think you are better than me. But you are dung. Less than that. You are the maggots that eat dung."

Lou gnawed on her lip, a habit in moments of stress. She dearly desired to understand. So as not to discourage him, she widened her smile and said, "Believe you me, you're in no danger so long as you cooperate. Truth is, for a red devil you're sort of cute."

Zach was dumbfounded. *Cute? The white boy had called him* cute?

Louisa snickered at her boldness. If her pa had ever heard her talk like that, he'd scold her for being a shameless hussy. But what harm was there, especially when the

Indian had no idea what she was saying? "I like that chin of yours. Square. Rugged. My grandma raised me to believe you can tell a person's character by the shape of their chin. What do you think?"

"I think your grandmother is an idiot and so are you," Zach said, still in Shoshone. Chins did not denote character. Any simpleton knew that. It was the shape of the ears that counted.

Clutching the sorrel's reins, then the lead rope, Lou bobbed her head at the top of the ridge. "Up and over we go. I'll be right behind you, so don't get any ideas."

Zach balked. He had gone to considerable effort to track the elk down, and was loathe to leave it unguarded. The scent of a fresh kill would attract every predator for miles around. By morning half the bull would be gone.

"What are you waiting for?" Lou asked. She feared he would raise a fuss and she would have to kill him. While she had shot practically every kind of game there was, she'd never slain a human being. So what if it was an Indian? Indians were flesh and blood, just as she was.

Zach came within a whisker of tucking at the waist and barreling into his captor. The flintlock deterred him; it might go off. Boiling like an untended pot, he stalked toward the crest. All that meat going to waste! What a shame!

Lou was tickled that the redskin had given in. Renewed confidence invigorated her as she trailed him. Exactly why she was so happy eluded her. Maybe it was having three extra horses now. Maybe it was capturing the Indian all by her lonesome. Or maybe—just maybe—she was happy because she had someone to talk to, even if it was a potential enemy.

A trapper's life was a lonely one. During all those weeks she and her pa were in that valley, they had not come across another living soul until the savages showed up. The work itself was downright grueling, backbreaking labor that winnowed out the weak from the strong, the determined from the dreamers. She had accompanied hcr pa many a morning, and always wound up utterly exhausted. How her father had abided the strenuous toil day in and day out was a mystery.

Or was it? Louisa remembered an evening when they had been relaxing after a day spent battling icy currents to set new traps. "I'm so sore I can barely move," she had complained.

"A little work never hurt anybody," her pa had said.

"You call what we did today a *little*? I hate to see what you'd call a lot."

"Always remember, daughter. No one can ford a river without getting wet."

Lou had grinned. Her pa was forever coming up with homey sayings, half of which made no sense. "Why ford it at all if there's a bridge handy?"

Zebulon had arched an eyebrow. "I swear. Sometimes you worry me, girl. You're always so set on taking the easy way out. In my day a body took sweat and aggravation in stride. It's the price we pay for going after our dreams."

"In your day? You make it sound as if you're a hundred years old, Pa."

"Truth to tell, I feel that old."

Something in his tone had made Lou look up. "You do?"

"Ever since your ma died I've felt downright ancient." Her father had peered into his battered tin coffee cup. "When you've lived forty winters like I have, maybe then you'll understand. I shouldn't say this, but there are days, child, when I'm tired of living. When I want to put a pistol in my mouth and end it."

"Pa!"

Zeb had shrugged. "Don't fret. I'm not about give up the ghost voluntarily." He'd winked. "Not while you're alive, anyhow."

Lou had been appalled. Her father had been despondent ever since her mother died, and who could blame him? But this? She had not known what to say or do to change his outlook, so she had joked, "In that case, you're never passing on. I aim to stick around a good long while. You'll be hobbling around on a cane before I die."

"You'd do that to me, wouldn't you?" Zeb had laughed, but the laughter had not touched his eyes. "It's my own fault, I reckon. It's what I get for giving birth to a woman as bullheaded as I am."

Taken aback, Louisa had felt herself flush. "That's the first time you've ever called me a woman, Pa. I'm not, though. I'm still a little girl."

"Sixteen is hardly little. You're as tall as your ma was. All you need to do is fill out some and you'll be her spitting image." He'd then developed an unusual interest in some pebbles near his foot.

"I'll never be as pretty as she was."

"You'll be prettier." Zeb had flicked one of the pebbles. "No, I can't lie to you, Lou. You'll always be rather plain. It's not your fault, though. We can't help how we're born. And being plain won't keep you from catching a fine man. Your ma snared me, didn't she?"

It was one of the tenderest moments they'd ever shared. Louisa had blushed a darker shade and responded, "I'm not interested in boys yet, Pa. You know that."

"You will be, soon enough. And when you start trolling for nibbles, don't settle for the first fish that takes the hook. Look around. Find yourself someone who will treat you decent. A man who loves you, heart and soul."

Lou had not been able to shed her embarrassment. Discussing intimate matters was rarely done, even when her mother was alive. "I'll do my best. But those days are still a ways off."

"Your ma wasn't much older than you when we met," her father had pointed out. Then, as if divining her discomfort, he'd chuckled and added, "Being plain has it benefits. You'd never have been able to pass yourself off as a boy if you were a raving beauty."

David Thompson

The ruse had been Louisa's brainstorm.

They had been in St. Louis, several days shy of departing, when they'd encountered a grizzled mountaineer fresh in from the Rockies. During a pleasant supper, the oldster had mentioned how scarce women were west of the Mississippi. White women, that is. And how white men flocked to them like bears to honey.

"You'd best be mighty careful, gal," the trapper had cautioned. "Being young won't keep the hounds from baying at your heels. When a man's in the mood, he'll move heaven and earth to soothe his craving."

It had been food for thought. The next day Lou had proposed posing as a boy to her father.

"It'll never work," he'd said.

"Why not? I'm plain enough to pass for one. You said so yourself. All it would take is some baggy clothes, and no one could tell the difference."

"Your voice would give you away."

"Why? It's deeper than most of the girls my age. So long as I don't let anyone hug me, I'll be safe."

Zeb had given in, with reservations. "Yep. Just like your ma. Once you set your mind to something, there's no changing it. We'll give your idea a try. If it works, fine and dandy. If it don't, I'll shoot the first son of a jackass who lays a finger on you."

Fortunately for the beaver brigade, the ploy had worked. No one had suspected the truth. Lou had been extremely careful not to let anyone get too close.

The only mistake she'd made had come during the Rendezvous. On the fourth day she had gone off to locate somewhere safe to wash up. A mile south of the encampment had been a secluded pool partly ringed by briars. She had stripped off her buckskins and had been wading in when she'd caught sight of someone else already in the water. Someone who'd had the same notion.

An Indian woman had been hunkered in the river up to her neck. A beautiful woman, with luxurious raven tresses and a full bosom. She had shocked Louisa by saying in flawless English, "Do not be alarmed. I am the wife of a trapper. You are most welcome to join me. The pool is big enough for the two of us."

"Pleased to meet you, ma'am," Lou had blurted out. "I didn't think I'd find anyone else so far down the Green."

"I like to bathe every day. This is one of the few safe spots. The men are too lazy to come all this way to relieve themselves."

Lou had cackled, then covered her mouth lest she be heard by a stray rider. "Sorry. But you sure have menfolk pegged."

The woman's lovely eyes had twinkled. "Red or white, it does not matter. They like to puff out their chests and strut like quail. They like to boast of their deeds in war. They will wrestle one another for hours, or run miles to win a footrace. But they will not take more than ten steps from their lodge to empty their bladders."

"Your husband is the same?"

"No. He does not like to sleep on the floor."

It had taken a bit to sink in, and when it had, Louisa had laughed for pure joy at the woman's frankness.

"I do not like to give advice unless it is asked for," the woman had said. "But for your sake, little one, I will share the secret of a long and happy marriage."

"What is it?" Lou had breathlessly inquired.

"Training."

"Ma'am?"

"Have you ever had a pet dog?"

"We've owned three. Two were big hounds killed by a nasty old bear. The third was a mongrel that followed us home from church one Sunday. Pa wanted to chase it off with a broom, but Ma had taken a shine to it. So I got to keep him. Rufus, we called him."

"Did you train Rufus to fetch? To sit?"

"Oh, I taught him to do all sorts of tricks. He would roll over and beg and hop on his hind legs."

"You must do the same with your husband. Train him early on to do the things he should. No matter how much he objects. It will spare you much heartache later on, when you have been together so long that you grate on each other's nerves."

"Don't you get along with your man?"

"Oh, yes, very much so." The Indian woman had moved toward the grassy bank. "But when I was a girl I would dream about taking a husband. I imagined he would be tall and handsome. That he would work day and night to please me. That he would do all the things he should without my having to nag. I imagined he would be perfect." She had glanced back and winked. "There is no such thing as a perfect man."

Out of shyness, Lou had averted her gaze when her new acquaintance rose up out of the water. "Thanks for chatting, ma'am. It was a pleasure to meet you."

"Call me Winona. I do not recall seeing you at the Rendezvous before. What is your name?"

Not until that moment had Louisa realized the woman was privy to her secret. Admitting who she was might land her in a heap of grief, if word got out. As much as she'd liked Winona, as much as she'd felt Winona could be trusted, she'd fibbed. Racking her brain, she'd blurted out the first name that popped into her head. "Abigail. I'm Abigail Adams. We got here a short while ago."

Winona had been about to don a fine buckskin dress. "Adams? One of the Great Fathers of your country had that name, did he not?" She'd begun to slip it on. "I'm sorry. You call them presidents. The one I am thinking of was called John, and he had a wife named Abigail."

Louisa had been stunned. "How in the world did you know that?"

"My husband has many books. Each evening he reads to us. I have learned much about your people and your government."

"My ma named me after Abigail Adams," Louisa had

explained, compounding her lie. Otherwise, Winona might have become suspicious.

"What does your name mean?"

Lou had had no idea. "I forget. How about yours?"

"One who gives."

"Gives what?"

Winona had smiled warmly. "One who gives of herself." She'd walked up the bank to the break in the briars. "I am honored to have met you, Abigail Adams. Remember, men often leave their shirts tucked out." On that enigmatic note, she had waved and left.

To this day, Louisa was unsure whether the woman had guessed the whole truth. Now, as she dogged the Indian youth's footsteps into the stand of trees, she regretted not learning which tribe Winona belonged to. Instinct had told her the woman would help her, and that she would feel more comfortable going to someone she knew rather than someone she had seen just once, and never talked to.

"Roost on that log yonder," Lou now commanded her captive, jabbing her pistol at it so he would catch on.

Zach simmered like a stew. He was tired of being tied up, tired of being bossed around. The moment the white boy lowered his guard, he would turn the tables. He sat on the end of the log, his body balanced on the balls of his feet.

Louisa deposited the meat near the fire, then slipped what was left of the rope from the sorrel's saddle horn. "I'm sorry. I'm not fond of having a blade stuck into me in the middle of the night. I've got to tie your legs, too."

Opening his mouth, Zach came close to telling her to go to Hell. Instead, he bowed his chin and drooped his shoulders as if all his spunk had fled.

Lou halted. Against her will she was beginning to feel sorry for him. He'd done her no harm, even when he could have. "Listen, Indian. Since we're going to be together a spell, the least we can do is make the best of it.

I'm Lou." Tapping her chest, she repeated it a number of times.

Zach could not have cared less. He was poised to lash out, to bowl the fool over and kick him senseless.

"What's your handle?" Louisa wanted to know. "Do you savvy?" She touched herself, then poked a thumb his way.

To humor the greenhorn, Zach gave his Shoshone name. "Stalking Coyote."

"Why are you heathens always named after animals and plants and such?" Lou asked. She unwound the rope, took another step, then stiffened as a lightning bolt ripped through her from head to toe. "English! That was English!"

Zach was as flabbergasted as she was. He'd made a boneheaded mistake and lost his advantage.

"You've been playing me for an idiot all along! You do speak our tongue!" Lou raised the pistol. "Why? What are you up to? Letting me babble while you kept quiet. I'd forgotten how sneaky you red vermin are."

Now that his ruse had been discovered, Zach saw no need to go on acting. "You've got your nerve, you bastard. I was minding my own business. You had no call to go waving a gun in my face."

Memories of her father's last moments tore at Louisa's heartstrings, threatening to tear them asunder. "How dare you!" And how could she have felt sorry for him? An Indian was responsible for Zeb's death! An Indian as devious and spiteful as Stalking Coyote! Not one of them was worth a handful of beans. Well, maybe one. Winona.

"Go ahead! Shoot!" Zach taunted. "It's just like a white cur to kill someone who is unarmed and hogtied."

"Enough!" Lou's arm was shaking. There was only so much a person could take!

Zach started to stand, heedless of the flintlock.

Louisa steadied her hand and took a deep breath. She had warned him and he hadn't listened. Now he had to die!

Chapter Four

At that exact moment, thirty miles to the north, in a picturesque cabin situated in a lush valley bordered by magnificent jagged peaks, a young girl paused in the doorway to declare, "I'm going down to the lake to see if the flowers have bloomed yet, Ma."

Winona King was mending a hunting shirt. Seated at a sturdy oak table built by her mate, she set the shirt down and glanced out the window. It would be dark in a couple of hours. "All right. But do not dawdle."

"I won't," Evelyn King promised. Picking flowers was a daily pastime of hers when they were in season. She loved flowers, loved how pretty they were, loved their scent, loved to decorate the cabin with them. Now that winter was about over, she was eager to begin collecting again.

"And keep your eyes peeled," Winona said. "Remember those wolf tracks we've been seeing."

Evelyn patted the leather bag slung over her left shoulder. "Don't fret, Ma. I have my pistol." It was a small flintlock, half the size of her father's, a gift from him on her last birthday.

"Still, you be careful. And leave the door open." From where she sat, Winona could see the lake off through the pines. Should she need to, she could reach it quickly.

"No silly wolf will bother me," Evelyn said, and merrily skipped across an open space to a well-worn trail. She hummed as she went, her arms swinging. After being cooped up in the cabin most of the day, she was happy to be out and about.

Winona resumed sewing. She was not unduly worried about the wolf. It was unusual for one to venture as close as this one had done, but it had not bothered their horses or the chickens she had acquired a year ago. Wolves generally shunned humans. And they were more apt to be abroad after dark than during the day. So her daughter should be safe.

The wolf was the farthest thing from little Evelyn's mind. She was enjoying how sunlight dappled the trail, and how the tall pines on both sides arched so high they seemed to brush the sky.

If anyone had asked Evelyn what one word best described her outlook on life, she would have said "happy." She was always happy. Happy she had a wonderful mother and father. Happy they lived in a cozy cabin. Happy their valley teemed with chipmunks and squirrels and birds to amuse and delight her. Happy, most of all, simply to be *alive*.

The only complaint Evelyn had with life was that the Great Mystery had seen fit to give her a brother. She would rather have had a sister. She and Zachary were forever squabbling, and had been ever since she was old enough to walk and talk. Her father assured her it was perfectly normal, but that did not make having to put up with Zach any easier.

Take their last fight, for instance. He had started it. All because she had taken a peek at his silly claw collection and lost one when she'd used it to dig in the dirt. Eagle claws were easy to come by. The Shoshones had enough to fill a bucket. But Zach had ranted and raved, saying she had no business touching his things when he was not there. Why, he'd even had the nerve to accuse her of being a thief! His own sister! Boys could be such pains, but brothers were worst of all.

At the moment Zach was gone, though, so all was right with the world. Evelyn saw a robin tugging at a big, fat worm, and giggled. She watched a gray squirrel leap from branch to branch at a dizzying height, and marveled that it didn't fall and break its neck. A chipmunk scolded her from the safety of a boulder, so she stuck her tongue out at it.

Then Evelyn was at the lake, standing on the shore with the wind whipping her hair. As always, ducks and geese swam gaily about or dived for fish.

A few gulls winged above, screeching like harpies. She used to feed them crumbs and such until one bit her hand hard enough to break the skin and draw blood. Ever since, they were her least favorite birds. Next to buzzards, of course. Buzzards had never done anything to hurt her; they were just plain ugly.

Evelyn skipped to the left, to where the first flowers could usually be found. To her utmost joy, some were in bloom. The blue ones. The ones she was named after.

Blue Flower was her Shoshone name. Everyone in the family had one. Zach was known as Stalking Coyote, which she thought was wrong. He should be called Stalking Skunk. Her father was known far and wide among many tribes as the fearless Grizzly Killer. Everyone said he had killed more of the great bears than any man alive, white or red. It made her proud. She was never afraid when he was around.

He had been gone, though, since early morning, off looking for that wolf. It had come around again the previous night. At daybreak her father had found its tracks out by the corral. A bad mistake on the wolf's part. Her pa never let anything hurt the horses. Any painter or bear or other meat-eater that showed too much interest in them usually wound up as a rug or a blanket or something.

Evelyn clasped a stem to pluck a flower. But she changed her mind. Too few were in bloom yet. She should wait until more were. Turning she watched a duck stretch its wings and shake as if it had the shivers. *Animals are so silly*. Except for the scary ones.

Mountain lions terrified her. Once, a big one had attacked her and her mother near that very spot. It had nearly killed them. Now and then she had awful dreams about it. She would see the huge cat slinking toward her, its curved claws digging into the earth. She would see its terrible teeth, and those piercing eyes. And just as it sprang, she would wake up in a sweat, scared out of her wits. On occasion she screamed, waking the whole family. Her ma would comfort her; her pa would make her tea. They never got mad. Zach did, though. He said she was acting ''just like a girl.'' Well, how else was she supposed to act? She *was* a girl.

Boys were so dumb.

Evelyn strayed eastward along the shore. She liked to find smooth, round stones and skip them on the water. Her brother had taught her how. One of the nicest things he had ever done.

She found one and threw it. Four skips, and it sank. Hoping to do better, she searched for another, for one that was flatter. The flat stones were always the best. Spotting a likely prospect, she pranced over and bent. Then gasped.

Imbedded in the soft soil at the lake's edge were the freshly made tracks of a huge wolf. It had to be the same wolf that had been skulking around their cabin. Evelyn straightened and scoured the forest. The wolf might be watching her at that very moment. She slipped a hand into her leather bag and palmed the pistol.

A jay was pecking at a pinecone. Several chipmunks were chasing one another. One of the gulls had alighted on the shore not ten feet away and was waiting for a morsel it would never get.

The wolf could not possibly be nearby, Evelyn decided. When predators were on the prowl, smaller creatures always hid. She picked up the stone, but instead of skipping it on the lake she hurled it at the gull, which took to the air with a squawk.

Evelyn's only regret was that she had no friends her own age to play with. Not there in the valley, anyway. Their nearest neighbor was Scott Kendall, who lived with his family about twenty miles to the south. The Kendalls had a girl, Vail Marie, who was a little younger than Evelyn was, and as sweet as peaches. But they did not get to see one another very often.

Shakespeare McNair lived about thirty miles to the north. Unfortunately, he and his wife did not have any children, and were too old to start having any.

There was another young couple, a pair her father had saved from hostiles. Nice folks, they had staked out a homestead on the prairie far below. They were planning to have kids, they claimed. But they were taking their sweet time about it. By the time they did, she would be old enough to have some of her own.

So at times, Evelyn felt quite lonely. Which was why she enjoyed the family's annual visits to the Shoshones. Each and every summer they would go and live with her mother's people. The village always teemed with children, and Evelyn had many close friends among them. One girl, Gray Dove, was her best friend in all the world. They always spent hours playing with their dolls or doing other fun things.

Evelyn was proud of her dolls. Her mother had made them. One was in the likeness of a Shoshone woman; another was a baby in a cradleboard. The last, at Evelyn's own request, was a trapper, a mountain man just like her pa. Her mother had even added a beard made of horsehair. Evelyn loved to have her dolls do the things her parents did. She would reenact whatever struck her fancy. What made it specially enjoyable was that her doll family, unlike her real one, did not have a *boy* to always cause trouble.

Evelyn would never admit it to her brother, but she did love him dearly. She was worried about him, too. Not long ago she had overheard her mother and father talking. They were upset that Zach did not seem to like white people much anymore. Her father, in particular, had been very sad.

So Evelyn has asked Zach about it. He'd told her that he was tired of whites always hating him for no reason. She'd come right out and said he was all wrong, that she had never seen whites acting that way. Zach had replied that she was too young to understand, but that one day she would, and on that day he would feel sorry for her. Why had he said such a strange thing?

Evelyn roved further along the lake. She was feeling brave. She could still see the trail to the cabin, and she still held her pistol. Her very own pistol. It had been one of the proudest days of her life when her folks had given it to her. As her pa had put it, "We trust you enough to know you will use it wisely."

Naturally, Zach had laughed and said she would probably blow her foot off. It was too bad she couldn't shoot him.

A shriek in the trees startled her. A redheaded woodpecker had taken wing, as if spooked. Evelyn saw it streak off, then saw a dark shape moving through the brush under the tree in which the woodpecker had been. Her breath caught in her throat. Whatever it was, it stood as high as she was.

Turning, Evelyn hurried toward the trail. The creature turned also, and shadowed her. When she went faster, it did. Her skin prickled as if from a heat rash, and fear sprouted, numbing her.

She was being stalked!

* * *

He was a big man with shoulders wider than most, his powerful frame rippling with corded muscle. Black hair and a black beard framed a rugged face, a face that had known much hardship, yet one that could radiate much softness. Scars from past battles with beasts and bestial men showed that here was someone to be reckoned with. Buckskins clothed him; knee-high moccasins covered his feet. An ammo pouch and powder horn were slanted crosswise across his chest. Matching pistols adorned his waist. In his right hand was a Hawken, and on the stock was a brass plate bearing an inscription: "From Samuel Hawken to his good friend, Nathaniel King. The Year of Our Lord 1832."

Nate King had many friends. Among the trapping fraternity he was as highly regarded as Jim Bridger and Joseph Walker. Like Bridger, he was always ready to lend a hand to those in need. Like Walker, he was one of the few mountaineers to have trekked all the way to the Pacific Ocean and back.

Among the Shoshones, the Crows, and the Flatheads, Nate King was as highly regarded as their most famed warriors. The exploits of Grizzly Killer were told and retold around campfires far and wide. Since he always talked with a straight tongue, and since he always treated all Indians as equals and not as inferiors, he had earned their highest and deepest respect.

Among the Blackfeet, the Piegans, and the Bloods he was also held in respect, but for an entirely different reason. He was their enemy, their mightiest adversary, the one white they had tried to slay again and again. They believed that the greatness of a people could be measured by the greatness of their enemies, so Nate King's greatness added luster to their own. The warrior who finally claimed his scalp would live in legend forever.

Now, on this brightly sunny afternoon, the man known as Grizzly Killer paused and knit his brow in deep thought. For the better part of the day he had been tracking the lone wolf that had taken a strange interest in his homestead. It had been two weeks since the first tracks appeared, down by the lake. He had not thought much of it at the time. Wolves passed through the valley routinely. So did grizzlies and cougars and wolverines. So long as they were only passing through, he didn't mind. It was when they lingered, when they developed a craving for horseflesh or posed a threat to his loved ones, that Nate either chased them off or shot them dead.

Life in the wilderness was not like life in the cities. Take New York City, where Nate had been born and raised. There, the worst a man had to worry about were footpads and 1863 robbers. And if he avoided the parts of the city where the ruffians were common, even they posed little danger. A man need not go around armed. He could rely on the constables to deal with the riffraff.

How different the untamed mountains were. Here, men and women alike had to be on their guard every minute of every day. Anyone who went around unarmed was asking for an early grave.

Footpads and robbers would be considered tame perils in comparison to fierce carnivores and war parties.

Nate did not mind having to take precautions. Being a walking armory had become second nature to him. And he had become accustomed to the stress of always worrying whether his loved ones would make it through each day. Even so, at times it got to him. At times he wondered if all of them would be better off moving back East, where they could live to ripe old ages.

Nate would never forget the first time he'd mentioned it to his wife. Winona had studied him as if to verify he were serious; then she'd done the last thing he'd expected. She'd laughed long and loud. He had not asked why. He'd known she would tell him when she was done, and he'd been right.

"You would have us live like prairie dogs?"

"Prairie dogs?"

"Yes. They live close together in narrow burrows. The same as those of your kind who live in cities. You have told me how it is. How your father's lodge almost touched the lodges of others, they were so close. How you could not take ten steps without being on land claimed by someone else.'' She had paused. ''You said it was like those pickles crammed in a barrel at Bent's Fort. Remember?''

Nate had speculated how it was that women could recollect every word a man ever said when a difference of opinion arose, but could never recall their own. ''Yes.''

Winona had gestured at the crown of snowcapped peaks that encircled their haven, at the azure sky, at the shimmering lake. ''Would you have us give up all this to be pickles?''

So much for Nate's idea.

Now he sighed and bent to the wolf tracks again. The beast had circled the cabin several times during the night, then paced near the corral. Oddly enough, the horses had not acted up, not even his black stallion, which he could always count on to raise a ruckus when a predator was in the vicinity.

From the corral, the tracks had led to the front door. Nate shuddered to think that while his family slept in blissful ignorance, the wolf had been sniffing at the jamb. Why? It was damned peculiar behavior.

The prints had borne to the north, through a belt of pines to low hills that flanked craggy heights. Nate hoped they would lead to the animal's lair, but the wolf had climbed to a bench and squatted a while. Perhaps to howl to attract others of its kind, although Nate had a hunch it was a loner, a wolf that shunned the society of other wolves and went on bloody killing sprees. Deranged, they did things no normal wolf would ever do.

Just as this one was doing.

Leaving the shelf, the wolf had gone to the southeast. Toward the lake. Nate followed the tracks, noting the wolf's gait, the depth of the impressions, the shape of the pads. Something about them nagged at the back of his mind. It was a possible he had seen them before. But he had come across so many in his widespread travels, he could not be sure.

The wolf had held to a steady lope. It had detoured once to investigate a marmot den. And again to inspect an area where a buck and several doe had bedded down.

Nate's thoughts wandered.

Of late he had taken to musing on how he would have turned out if he'd stayed in New York. Would he be a bookkeeper, as he had once planned? Would he, day after day, be slaving away at a tiny desk over a musty ledger? Working himself into an early grave for a miser who wrung every minute's worth of effort out of employees treated as slaves? If his uncle had never written him and asked him to come West, would he still be languishing in a prison of his own making? Or would he have come to his senses anyway? He liked to believe so. But it might be wishful thinking.

Sad to say, most folks got into a rut and stayed there. They lived in quiet desperation, forever yearning for a better life, but never able to claw up out of the holes they had fallen into. They accepted what life handed them, without complaint.

Not Nate. Even as a child, he had dreamed of something better. All those years under his father's heel had not dimmed the hope that burned at his core. The hope that one day he would live free, to do as he wanted, where he wanted, when he wanted.

And that day had come. Thanks to his Uncle Zeke, who'd lured him West under false pretenses, he now enjoyed the kind of life he had always dreamed about. No one told him what to do. No one was constantly looking over his shoulder. No one would ever boss him around again.

Except Winona. But wives didn't count. They had a God-given right to wrap their husbands around their little fingers. It said so right in Scripture: *"Therefore shall a man leave his father and his mother, and shall cleave unto his wife; and they shall be one flesh."*

Shakespeare had reminded him of that one night many years ago. Nate had been peeved because Winona wanted him to build a woodshed at the rear of the cabin. "What's wrong with just stacking the limbs outside the door, like we've always done?" he had complained. "It'll take me two days to build a shed the size she wants."

McNair had taken a twig from his mouth and chuckled. "Then it will be two days well spent. Think how happy she'll be."

"For how long? Until she comes up with something else for me to do. She's never satisfied."

His mentor and dearest friend had shaken his head. "Women never are. Son, you've only been married a year. So I reckon you haven't realized yet that females are the spurs that prod us males into bettering our lives in spite of ourselves."

"Balderdash."

"You have a noble and true conceit," McNair had quoted. "Most men do. They think they should be the lords and masters of their castles. But in Proverbs it says, 'Every wise woman buildeth her house.' So don't hold it against Winona if she's doing what she was created to do."

"Oh? And what are men created to do?"

"Act pigheaded."

Nate had laughed.

" 'All the world's a stage. And all the men and women merely players. They have their exists and their entrances. And one man in his time plays many parts.' " Shakespeare had grown wistful. "His acts being seven ages. At first the infant, mewling and puking in his nurse's arms. Then the whining schoolboy, with his satchel and shining morning face, creeping like a snail unwillingly to school."

"Don't forget the canings," Nate quipped. "I never will."

Shakespeare had gone on, quoting. "Then the lover,

sighing like a furnace, with a woeful ballad made to his mistress's eyebrow.''

"Or her heart.''

"Aye. Then a soldier, full of strange oaths, and bearded like the pard, jealous in honor, sudden and quick in quarrel, seeking the bubble reputation even in the cannon's mouth.''

Nate had thought of his grandfather, who had been a ranger during the revolution against the British.

"Then the justice, in fair round belly with good capon lined, with eyes severe and beard of formal cut, full of wise saws and modern instances.''

"What next? Old age?''

"We're not quite there yet. No. The sixth age shifts into the lean and slipper'd pantaloon. With spectacles on nose and pouch on side. His youthful hose, well saved, a world too wide for his shrunk shank. And his big manly voice, turning again toward childish treble, pipes and whistles in his sound.''

"Your Bard could be a depressing gent.''

"I'm not done.'' Shakespeare had stroked his own beard a moment. "The last scene of all, that ends this strange eventful history, is second childishness and mere oblivion, sans teeth, sans eyes, sans taste, sans every thing.''

Nate had glanced sharply at the older man. "Oblivion? Is that what you believe your own self?''

"No, I must confess. But remember. That is one of old William S.'s characters speaking, not the Bard himself. As for me''—McNair had gazed at the sparkling stars— "we have a building of God, a house not made with hands, eternal in the heavens.''

Nate often wished he could recite from books as readily as his mentor. Shakespeare had a rare gift, the ability to remember, perfectly, everything he ever read. Whether it was the Complete Works of William Shakespeare, the Holy Bible, or a book of verse, Shakespeare never forgot a word.

Nate never ceased to be amazed by his friend's brilliance. McNair had missed his calling. A man with his flair for memory should have been a professor at a university. Nate had mentioned it once, and been surprised when Shakespeare agreed with him for once.

"It's the only regret I have about my life. When I was your age, I loved books. Could never get enough of them. I would rather read than eat or sleep. And at one point I seriously thought about becoming a teacher and passing on my love to fertile young minds."

"But?"

"But those books had fired my imagination too much. They had filled me with a hankering to see more of the world they painted so vividly. I had to go off and explore it for myself. So I traveled West, where no one had ever gone before. Long before beaver became all the rage. Long before most whites had ever set foot west of the Mississippi."

"Even long before Lewis and Clark," Nate had mentioned.

"Implying I'm as old as sin?"

"Not quite. You've got more wrinkles than a prune, but you weren't around at the Garden of Eden."

"Damn right I wasn't! I'd have told Satan to go jump in a creek." Shakespeare had clapped Nate on the shoulder. "Just think! Adam had everything any man ever wanted. All the food he could want was his for the taking. A beautiful naked woman waited on him hand and foot. He didn't have to build woodsheds, or mend roofs, or repair bridles. Hell, he didn't have to do any work at all. And what happened? He got himself kicked out of Paradise because he had the willpower of a chipmunk. He didn't know how to say no!"

"But it was Eve who ate of the forbidden fruit first."

"Oh, please. Spare me. She was tricked by the liar of all liars, Satan himself. All those who like to blame women for mankind's fall ought to remember that Eve was pushed."

Nate had changed the subject. When it came to debating religion or literature, he was no match for McNair. No one was. Shakespeare could talk rings around a tree, citing chapter and verse to prove his points.

A wall of brush brought Nate back to the present. The wolf had gone straight on through, but Nate slanted to the right to go around, confident he could pick up the trail again on the other side. By now he was so close to the lake that he could hear tiny waves lapping at the shoreline. As he came to the end of the thicket he heard something else, something that sent a shiver down his spine and galvanized him into racing toward the source.

It was a scream.

The scream of a child in mortal terror.

Chapter Five

Louisa May Clark trained the muzzle of her pistol on the center of the Indian's forehead and girded herself to squeeze the trigger. She had never killed before, though, and for a fraction of an instant she hesitated, summoning the courage to go through with it. And in that instant, two disturbing revelations gave her further pause. First, she saw that the Indian was not going to attack her; he was just mad. Second, she discovered something she had overlooked before. "Your eyes are green!"

In his fury Zach did not guess the leap of logic she had made. "Yes? So?"

"So you must be part white!" Lou knew that Indians always had dark eyes. Or almost always. The Mandans, her pa had revealed, were rumored to have fair-eyed babies now and again. They were exceptions to the rule—the only exceptions, so far as she knew.

And now that Lou studied her captive closely, she realized his features did indeed have a white cast. His jawline, his cheeks, his complexion, all bore the stamp of a white heritage. She had been fooled by the clothes he wore, and by the darkness of his skin. Skin burned brown by daily exposure to the sun, and weathered by the elements. She lowered the flintlock. "You are, aren't you?"

"What if I am?" Zach countered. "What difference does it make? You still had no call to treat me as you've done."

"I thought you were going to harm me," Lou confessed.

"White boys!" Zach scoffed. "Always so quick to think all Indians are bloodthirsty killers." He was so sick and tired of their bigotry, he could scream.

"Some Indians are killers," Lou said, but she did not elaborate. She could not bring herself to talk about the tragedy, not yet, not when it was so fresh in her memory, so horribly vivid.

"And so are some whites!" Zach retorted, pent-up venom gushing from him like steam from a geyser. "I know a trapper who has a tobacco pouch made from the breast of a Blackfoot woman. And another mountaineer who likes to boast of the time he killed and scalped an entire Lakota family. So don't stand there and try to convince *me* that whites are any better than Indians!"

Lou recoiled, stunned by the violence of his outburst. His face was red, his veins bulging, pure hatred in his eyes. For a second she thought he would spring on her, but he trembled slightly, took a deep breath, and regained control.

Zach regretted his lapse. Now the boy would mistrust him more than ever. To make amends, he said, "I'm a mite touchy about my mixed blood. But I give you my word that I'm no threat to you whatsoever. Cut me loose and I'll go my own way. You'll never see me again. I promise."

"You really expect me to believe you?" Lou said. How could she? Considering his hatred of whites, she felt safer keeping him bound.

The venom boiled to the surface again. "Oh. How

could I forget? I'm part Indian. That makes me evil, doesn't it? Everything I say must be an out-and-out lie.''

"I didn't say that.''

"You sure as hell did, boy.''

"Quit calling me that.''

"Why? Because I'm not much older than you.''

No, because I'm a girl! Louisa came close to shouting, but didn't. "Why don't you sit back down and calm yourself while I decide what to do.''

Zach would rather have taken that pistol and crammed it down the white's throat, but he obliged. Only by proving he was not a menace would he be released. He couldn't keep himself from glaring, though, so he stared into the distance instead. Gradually, his hot blood cooled. He cleared his throat. "Listen, we don't have to be enemies. You made a mistake. I made a mistake. Let's forgive and forget. Go our separate ways. How about it?''

Lou remembered how Stalking Coyote had not harmed her when he'd spied on her camp, and she was inclined to do as he wanted. Then she thought of her father. And of how treacherous the red race could be. "Tell me more about yourself.''

"What in the world for?''

"It will help me make up my mind.''

Zach thought he saw why. "Oh. You're worried I'm a Blackfoot or a Blood. Well, I'm not. My mother is Shoshone; my father is a white man.''

"Shoshone?'' Lou repeated. According to a few of the trappers she had jawed with at the last Rendezvous, the Shoshones were the friendliest tribe around. The tribe had never made war on whites, never so much as lifted a hand in anger against them. Why, then, was Stalking Coyote so filled with hate? Could he be lying? "Can you prove you are a Shoshone?''

"Prove it?'' Zach could not believe what he was hearing. "If you weren't so dumb, you'd know it by the style of my hair and my clothes.'' He snorted like a riled bull.

"How long have you been in the mountains anyway? Two days?"

Lou stamped a foot. "Why do you persist in making me mad? I should shoot you and be done with it. But I'm too nice a"—she almost said "girl"—"person to kill you without good cause. Just don't prod me, Indian."

Zach had had enough. "Untie me," he commanded, shoving his forearms toward her. "And be quick a-bout it."

If there was one thing Lou despised more than anything else, it was being *told* to do something against her will. Since she had been old enough to toddle, she had resented being given orders. Her mother had once commented that she was as "contrary as a cat with a thorn in its paw." If so, she came by her rebellious streak honestly, for her pa had jested on more than one occasion said that her ma was "born uppity, but adorable."

"No. I will not."

"Damn you! Why?"

"I still don't trust you," Louisa confessed.

Zach yearned to tear the flintlock from the boy's grasp and beat him over the noggin with it. Only, he had to concede the white youth had a point. He had done nothing to earn the boy's respect. Quite the opposite. "What, then? I'm to be kept tied until you feel you can?"

Lou did not see any other way. "I'm sorry. For now, yes." She shrugged. "Maybe by morning, provided you behave."

"Damn!" Zach spat, and slumped to the ground with his back to the log. This was what he got for being reasonable. He should have made his move back up on the ridge.

"My last name is Clark," Lou said, to spark conversation. It was nice to have someone to talk to, even if it was someone who looked as if he wanted to tear her limb from limb.

"Tell it to someone who cares."

Lou had never met anyone so blockheaded in all her

born days. "You're doing it again. I'm trying to be polite and you're throwing it in my face. Can't you at least pretend to be civil? I'll be more apt to take you at your word if you weren't always foaming at the mouth. Instead of Stalking Coyote, they should have named you Rabid Wolf."

Despite himself, Zach grinned. "My ornery excuse for a little sister says it should be Stalking Skunk."

"Oh! You have a sister?" Lou was glad. Somehow, it made the Indian youth seem more . . . human. "What is her name?"

Zach was slow in answering. To reveal the family's Christian name might come back to haunt him later, if word got out that he had let himself be taken by surprise by a greenhorn. Some of the mountaineers would rib him without mercy. "Blue Flower."

"How do you say it in Shoshone?" Lou listened closely, but she could not pronounce it quite right, which, much to her irritation, amused her prisoner. "What are you smirking at? I'll bet you didn't learn the white man's tongue overnight."

"I could speak it and the Shoshone language by my third birthday," Zach boasted. He had his mother's aptitude for acquiring new languages. "I also know some Spanish, some Flathead, some Cheyenne, and enough Nez Percé to get by."

"Mighty fond of yourself, aren't you?" Lou said, impressed, but refusing to further inflate his swollen head.

"I was just stating facts."

"Do you think I came down with the last rain?" Lou joked. "I've met scoundrels like you before. As high on themselves as a Georgia pine."

"Scoundrels?"

"Just a figure of speech."

"Is 'cute' a figure of speech, too?"

Lou had forgotten all about what she had called him. Unless she exercised extreme caution, he might suspect the truth. Laughing as if she did not have a care in creation, she responded, "You thought I said you were cute? Are you addlepated? I said that you looked like a newt. Your chin, your cheeks, they remind me of a slimy, slippery critter."

A blatant lie if ever Zach heard one. He didn't press the issue, but he could not sit there and let it go unchallenged. "If you say so. You have no room to talk, though. Your whole face is smooth enough to pass for a girl's. Anyone ever tell you that?" Among the Shoshones, to call a boy a girl was like slapping them. He hoped the insult would nettle Clark; it did much more. The white youth became beet red and staggered back as if he *had* been struck.

Louisa's heart fluttered madly. Was he teasing her? Did he know? She looked down at herself, at the baggy buckskins that hid her figure. No, he couldn't possibly. She relaxed a smidgen.

What was that all about? Zach wondered. Whites were so strange!

"I'll fix supper. You sit there and don't move," Lou directed. Anxious to keep busy, she hunkered by the fire and carved the elk meat into smaller pieces, arranging them on her makeshift spit. Partially roasted bits of rabbit lay on a flat piece of bark, where she had left them when she ran off in pursuit of the Shoshone. They would keep for breakfast.

Her stomach rumbled like a volcano. She was famished. Her appetite had returned with a vengeance. She could probably eat the whole slab by herself. Hungrily, she watched as the flames licked at the tantalizing morsels. She also watched Stalking Coyote, without being obvious. He truly was a handsome devil. And she did not know which amazed her more, that he was, or that she was attracted to him.

What was the matter with her? Lou chided herself. Just a few days ago Indians had murdered her father. Now here she was, making cow eyes at one! Someone should smack her over the head with a hammer to restore her senses!

"What are you grinning at?" he demanded.

Lou had not realized she was. Frowning, she said gruffly, "Just got some smoke in my eyes, is all."

Zach had resolved to make the best of a rotten situation. A little friendly talk might go a long way toward getting him cut free. And the sooner he was shed of the greenhorn, the better he would like it. "How long have you been in the mountains?" he inquired.

"Pretty near a year."

"That long?" Zach did not hide his surprise. Whites who had survived a winter in the high country were in a special class by themselves. Hivermen, they were called. Ordinarily, they were much more knowledgeable about wilderness lore than Lou Clark appeared to be.

"Why do you sound so shocked?" she asked.

"Do I?" Zach hedged. A whinny by one of the horses reminded him of something else. "Where's your partner? Off hunting?"

Lou was about to break a twig and add it to the fire. She paused. "What makes you think I have one?"

"Do you always answer a question with a question?" Zach rejoined. His mother had the same annoying habit when they were arguing. He nodded at the saddles. "It doesn't take a genius to figure out there are two of you."

"Oh." Lou snapped the dry twig. To deny the evidence of their own eyes was pointless. "Yes, I had a partner. He was killed. By your kind."

"Shoshones have never slain a white man."

Lou's eyes moistened. She would not look at him. "You know what I mean. He was rubbed out by Indians. A war party caught us, put an arrow into him." Her voice broke. Mentally, she cursed all the red men who had ever lived and ever would.

To be polite Zach said, "I'm sorry, boy."

"No, you're not. You never even met him."

"If it's any consolation, Clark, it happens all the time.

67

Out of every hundred baby-faced kids like you who come
to these mountains with dreams of making it rich in the
beaver trade, maybe ten live to recross the Mississippi.''
Zach was quoting his pa. Shakespeare McNair was of the
opinion the survival rate was much lower.

Lou was offended. He was treating her father like
some kind of statistic! ''It's no consolation at all, Shoshone. My pa was the kindest man who ever donned
britches. He always treated me decent. Treated everyone
decent. It was wrong for him to meet his end as he did.''

''It was your father? You didn't say.''

''Now you know.''

''The Lord giveth, and the Lord taketh away,'' was all
Zach could think of to say.

''What?''

''From scripture,'' Zach said. One of the few passages
he remembered, and then only because Shakespeare was
so fond of quoting it.

''Is that supposed to make me feel better?'' Louisa
said testily. ''The Lord had no business taking my pa
from me. Why are we born anyway? Why are we given
life in the first place? Just to die? To be struck down in
our prime at the whim of foul red butchers?''

''White men kill, too.''

Lou gripped a stick so hard, her knuckles were white.
''So? No one should kill! Ever! Why can't we all live
together in peace and brotherhood? Why is there always
so much spite? So much bloodshed?'' She rose, rife with
indignation. ''I used to think the Almighty watched over
each and every one of us. Just like he does the sparrows.
But now I've seen the light. We're nothing to him. How
else could he let us suffer? How else could he let a decent
man like my pa die, choking on his own blood?'' She
fought back tears. ''We're bugs. That's what we are.
Tiny bugs who scurry around our tiny world, no-account
ants beneath his notice.''

The intensity of the youth's verbal storm jolted Zach.

He imagined how he would feel if it had been his pa, and sympathy blossomed.

Lou tilted her head to the darkening twilight. "Why?" she railed at the heavens. "Why did it have to be him? Why couldn't you take me instead?" A storm cloud inside her split wide and a torrent gushed forth. Unwilling to let the Indian see her cry, she dashed into the trees, her arms over her face.

Zach rose, but was at a loss as to what to do. Some things a man had to deal with himself, as his pa would say. Racking sobs came from the brush, high-pitched sobs more becoming of someone Evelyn's age than his own. He sagged against the log to wait for Clark to come back.

What was he doing? Zach straightened. The stripling had left the butcher knife on a rock by the fire. His Hawken and his flintlocks were on a blanket nearby. How peculiar that he should feel guilty about doing what he did next! Which was to slice his bounds, arm himself, and sit by the end of the log. He laid the rifle, knife, and rope on the ground.

The sobbing went on forever. Zach could have taken his horses and ridden out, and Lou Clark would have been none the wiser. But it was as plain as the nose on his face that the white youth was not in any shape to be traipsing through the wilderness alone. The boy would get himself killed, for sure. So Zach planned on taking Clark with him. His father would see to it the boy reached St. Louis in one piece.

Zach surprised himself. He thought poorly of whites, yet here he was, going out of his way to help one. Wasn't that what folks called being a hypocrite? Maybe not. His mother and father, both, had long taught that a person should always help others in need.

His attention perked. The sobbing had dwindled to random groans. Soon the boy would reappear. Clasping his hands as if they were still bound, he raised his knees so Clark would not spot the pistols. Footsteps crunched on dry leaves. Soon Clark emerged, a study in human misery.

Louisa hung her head, too sad to care what the Shoshone might think. She had needed a good cry. It was just more cruel injustice that she'd broken down in the presence of a heathen. Suddenly, she did not want him around any longer. He was a constant reminder of her father's fate—and of those who were to blame for that fate. She was of a mind to cut Stalking Coyote loose and set him on about his own business.

She would rather be alone anyway.

Lou went to the fire. She did not look at the Indian because she did not want him privy to the depths of her sorrow. "Glad I got that out of my system," she announced harshly. "Now where were we?"

"You were just about to put down your guns and raise your hands."

Whirling, Lou found herself staring into the muzzle of the Shoshone's rifle. She glanced at the blanket and did something ladies rarely did. She swore. "Damn!"

Zach reasoned it was smarter to disarm the youth. It would lessen problems later on, and he would not have to worry about a slug in the back on the long ride home. "Set them down, real easy-like. And don't do anything rambunctious. For your own sake."

Lou would do no such thing. Once unarmed, she would be completely at his mercy. And how did she know he truly was a Shoshone? Maybe he was lying. Maybe he was a canny hostile who would do all those wicked things Indians were rumored to do to female captives. "I can't."

"Can't or won't?" Zach was in no mood to be bucked. "I give you my promise that you'll come to no harm."

"And you expect me to believe you?" Lou laughed icily. "When cows sprout wings and fly." Her hands inched toward her flintlocks.

Zach leaped erect. "Don't do anything rash." He had not anticipated this. But he should have. How often had

Shakespeare McNair mentioned that "desperate people are always the most dangerous. When a coon has nothing to lose, son, that's when he'll risk it all."

"I'm tired," Lou said, continuing to creep her fingers higher.

"So am I. We each need a good night's sleep." Zach moved forward slowly so as not to scare the boy into doing something they would both regret.

Lou's lips curled in a lopsided sneer. The Shoshone didn't understand. She was tired, all right, but tired *of living*. With her father and mother gone, life had lost its value. It was too ridiculous for words. Too barbarous. She wanted no part of it. No part of a ruthless world ruled by a stonehearted God who was deaf to the appeals of his own creatures. She would rather join her mother and father in the next life, if there even was a "next life."

Zach was eight feet away. He did not want to shoot, but he might have to. Clark's expression was ample proof. Wild, wide-eyed, like the fierce visage of a cornered beast. But another emotion was at work, an emotion Zach could not quite identify. "I've no hankering to harm you," he reiterated.

The statement tickled Lou's funny bone. In a world of madmen, she would qualify as one of the maddest if she accepted him at his word. Indian warriors lived for one thing, and one thing alone. Counting coup. To earn glory in war, to slay many enemies, to steal many horses, these were the standards by which Indian youths like Stalking Coyote were measured. She tensed, and grinned.

Zach was not close enough to stop Clark from drawing. No one would blame him if he fired. It was his life or the white youth's, and he was not partial to dying so young. Clark's tear-streaked cheeks induced him to make a final appeal. "Please, Lou. For both our sakes."

"I'm sorry, Stalking Coyote. I'm so tired." Louisa had to blink to clear her vision. "I'm at the end of my rope. I'd rather end it." Her hands stabbed for the flintlocks.

Zachary could never say what made him do what he

71

did next. A tap on the trigger would have sufficed. But he leaped to one side even as he reversed his grip on the Hawken and swung it like a club. A pistol boomed, spewing lead and smoke. He felt a tug on his shirt. Then the Hawken's stock caught Clark on the chin as the white youth raised the other flintlock, and Lou Clark folded like a crumpled piece of paper, to lie in a heap.

"Danged jackass!" Zach said, and swiftly bent to claim the pistols. He need not have worried. The white boy was unconscious. Zach let the guns be and slipped his arm under Clark to carry him to the log. It was like lifting a feather. The buckskins sagged like so much extra skin.

"No wonder you wanted elk meat," Zach said to himself. The boy needed fattening up. Zach placed Clark next to the pile of rope. By tying the short pieces into one long one, he had enough to bind the white's wrists. He had to roll Clark onto a hip to grab Clark's left arm. As he did, Clark's body rolled against his. Against his right hand.

Zach bounded backward as if he had brushed against a scorpion. Astounded, he gingerly reached out and lowered his palm to a specific spot high on Clark's chest. "My God!" he breathed. His palm traveled to a corresponding spot on the other side. "It can't be!" Squatting, he examined the white nose to nose.

Little details he had missed now leaped out at him. The shape of the lips. The dainty ears. In a swirl of confusion, Zach sat back on his haunches to ponder, blurting out, "It's a *girl!*" How could he have been so blind? So stupid?

She moaned, and Zach cast the rope from him as if it were a sidewinder. Scooting to the fire, he sat cross-legged. He had no water to dash on her face. And the stream was too far off to leave her unguarded. He would wait for Clark to revive. She should be all right; he hadn't hit her hard enough to gravely hurt her. He hoped.

Zach stared at the limp figure. She was unlike most

white girls he'd met. By and large, they were dainty wisps in frilled clothes who would as soon gargle with broken glass as live in the wilds. Clark was different. She could live off the land. She dressed like a boy, she fought like a boy. Qualities no other girl he'd ever met possessed. Even Shoshone girls liked their frills, their beads and decorated buckskin dresses and whatnot.

Zach had never thought he would see the day when a *girl* could sneak up on him, could take him prisoner and bind him. She was brave, as well as clever. The traits of a warrior. He liked that.

Clark stirred, but did not yet awaken. Zach had a silly impulse to go over and rest her head in his lap. Instead, he checked his guns. Every few seconds he would glance at her. She was rather ordinary. But he liked the way her upper lip puckered outward, and the way her eyebrows were arched in the center. Her throat bobbed, and so did his.

"Ohhhhh." Louisa sat bolt upright, befuddled but remembering she had been in a clash with—who? She spotted the Shoshone by the fire. "You!" she exclaimed, and clawed for flintlocks that were not there.

"Why didn't you tell me?"

"Tell you what?" Lou spied her weapons and began to rise, but the Shoshone youth's reply seared her motionless.

"Why didn't you tell me you were female?"

Louisa scrambled back against the log, then up into a crouch. She was prepared for the worst. "You know? How?"

Zach did not have to see his own face to know he blushed. Averting his gaze, he said, "It's enough that I do. I wish you had told me from the start. I would not have raised the fuss I did."

"What will you do with me now?"

Her anxiety aroused Zach's pity. To soothe her, he attempted to make her laugh. "What else?" he said, light-heartedly. "I'll truss you up and drag you off to my village."

Louisa had feared as much. She would not end her days as the unwilling mate of any man. Her fingers wrapped around the butcher knife that had been carelessly left lying next to the log, and she placed all her weight on her hind leg. "Like hell you will!" Surging upright, she arced her arm around, throwing the weapon as her father had taught her, as she had practiced daily for the past year. It flew true—straight at the chest of Stalking Coyote.

Chapter Six

I won't panic! I won't panic! I won't panic! Little Evelyn King mentally yelled at herself as she moved briskly toward the trail to the cabin. Briskly, but she did not run. Her father had told her she must never flee from a nasty old predator. The big cats and wolves and such were used to chasing prey down. When something ran from them, they automatically ran after it.

If a meat-eater was already charging her, that was different. Then, fleeing might be the only way to save her life.

"This doesn't count for grizzlies," her pa had explained. "They're just too unpredictable. Whether you stand still or run won't matter to them. It all depends on what kind of mood they're in."

"Why are they so different from the rest?" she had asked.

"Because they're not afraid of anything. Silvertips are the only animals in all creation which don't know the meaning of fear."

"How can that be, Pa?"

"They're so big and strong, they can kill any creature that lives. Even buffalo. So they see themselves as the lords of their domain."

"They're just plain mean," Evelyn had said.

Her father had smiled and rested a brawny hand on her shoulder. "Never blame an animal for being true to its nature. Predators survive by killing. That's what they're good at. And grizzlies are best of all at what they do."

"They kill people, too. If that's not mean, what is?"

"To them we're just another kind of food. And once they find out how easy we are to kill, they make it a point to hunt us down."

It had been her turn to laugh. "Easy to kill? You? Pa, you're the toughest man alive. Even Uncle Shakespeare says so."

"We might like to think we are. But compared to a grizzly, people are downright puny. Without a rifle and two pistols and a butcher knife, we're as easy to kill as helpless baby birds. And predators would rather kill prey that can't hurt them than prey that can."

"Why did God do that, you reckon?"

"Do what?"

"Make us so puny? Shouldn't it be the other way around?"

"Maybe it's God's way of keeping us humble. Trust me. Have a bear try to eat you just once, and you'll never be too big for your britches ever again."

She had giggled. "You've tangled with silvertips whole bunches of times. That must make you the humblest man alive, Pa."

"Just remember my advice, little one. Never run, unless you can't help it. And then run like hell."

"Pa! You used a naughty word! I'm going to tell Ma."

A low sound from the brush ended Evelyn's recollection. It was not a growl, exactly. Or a snarl. More like a rumbling grunt, if that were possible. She could see the dark shape keeping pace with her. It wound through the undergrowth with an ease born of long experience.

Her only hope lay in reaching the cabin. Or in getting close enough to holler for her mother.

Evelyn clutched her pistol to her chest. She tried to recall the last time she had checked to verify it was loaded, and couldn't. A misfire would spell her doom. If people were puny, she was one of the puniest, being so young and so small and all. Whatever was stalking her would gobble her down in a few big bites.

Evelyn could not wait to grow up. To be an adult. She would always wear two pistols, like her pa, and carry a rifle wherever she went, like both her parents did. Some of the trappers had poked fun at her father when he'd taught her mother how to shoot and bought her ma some guns. But her pa had been right to do so. Several times now her mother had saved their lives because of it.

Another rumbling sound drew Evelyn's gaze to the beast. She had been trying not to think about it, hoping it would simply go away. Instead, it was closer now, angling slowly toward her.

She remembered her pa's other advice. "Never turn your back on a meat-eater. If all else fails, try to stare them down. Sometimes that will make them back off."

"Why?"

"I don't rightly know. Some of the mountaineers believe that the Good Lord made us masters of all the creatures on Earth, so all we have to do is look at them and they will bend to our will."

"That's silly. Whoever said that never owned a kitten."

The thing in the bushes was now within springing range. It was just on the other side of some high weeds. Evelyn extended her small pistol and thumbed the hammer back as she had been instructed. Her legs were quaking. Her teeth started to chatter so she grit them tight.

I will not panic! I will not panic!

The weeds rustled. Through them poked a dark snout.

Black nostrils flared, sniffing loudly. Part of a large head appeared. Hairy, with pointed ears. Thin lips curled up over tapered teeth, teeth as long as Evelyn's fingers. The tip of a tongue jutted out.

It was a wolf. One of the biggest she had ever seen. She aimed the flintlock at its head, then recalled her father saying that an animal's skull was the thickest bone in its body. Head shots were seldom deadly unless a large-caliber gun was used. Hers was only a .32.

"Go for the heart or the lungs," her pa had advised. Which was all well and good if the animal was standing sideways. But what was she to do when it was facing her head-on, like this wolf?

Licking her dry lips, Evelyn said, "Why don't you step on out here, you varmint. Try to take a bite out of me and see what happens."

The meat-eater tilted its head and sniffed even louder. Piercing eyes fixed on her as if to devour her alive.

I will not panic! I will not panic! Evelyn thought it over and over, but her legs were quaking worse than ever, and it felt as if a swarm of butterflies were loose in her stomach. It was like the time the mountain lion had attacked. Only worse. Because then she had been so worried about her mother, she had given little thought to her own safety. So she had not been quite as scared.

The wolf slid on into the open, long body slung low to the ground, knobby paws splayed. Evelyn still could not get a good shot at its chest. She sidestepped, placing each foot down carefully for fear of her legs giving out. The pistol commenced to shake. *No! No! No!* she railed at herself. She must stay calm!

The wolf's sleek form rippled with corded muscle. Its tail was held straight out, just as her pa said wolves did when they were about to charge. Claws that could rip her wide open now dug into the earth for purchase.

Evelyn could not help herself. She tried to be brave. She tried to do as her ma and pa would do. But ravaging terror seized her. And before she could stop herself, she had done the one thing she had promised herself she would never do in times of danger. She screamed.

As if on signal, the wolf sprang. Evelyn banged off a shot, but her hands were trembling so badly that the lead ball intended for the predator's chest plowed instead into the soil. The wolf loomed above her. She flung her arms up to ward it off, stumbling backward as she did. A rock snagged her heel, and flung off balance, she fell. Flailing her arms to regain her balance did no good.

Evelyn landed on her back. She tried to jump up, but the wolf was on her in a flash, straddling her, its great head poised above hers. She saw its teeth, saw the maw part to bite, saw its tongue extend further.

The wolf licked her.

About to scream again, Evelyn froze. *It had licked her?* The beast did so again, its slick tongue sliding over her cheeks, her chin, her neck. It whined deep in its throat the whole while. Evelyn blinked, looked deep into its eyes, and suddenly knew the truth. She went to fling her arms around its neck.

Abruptly, above them both, towered a living mountain of righteous wrath, a butcher knife aloft for a fatal thrust.

"No, Pa!" Evelyn screeched. "It's Blaze!"

Nate King had burst from the woods to see a huge wolf on top of his beloved daughter. Since a bullet might go completely through the animal and strike her, he had resorted to his knife. Now, his every sinew vibrating with the urgent need to kill, he saw a wide white blaze on top of the wolf's head, and heard his daughter yell.

The keen blade did not descend. "Blaze?" Nate said in astonishment, and slowly lowered his arm. The wolf turned, rising on its rear legs so it could lick at his face.

Evelyn stood, laughing in relief and joy. "Zach's old friend has come back to pay us a visit!"

Nate had almost forgotten about the cub his son had rescued and kept as a pet. It had left years ago to be with its own kind, and the boy had cried and cried. To Nate's surprise, the wolf did come back from time to time, always for shorter and shorter periods. The last visit had been ages ago. Nate had assumed it was long since worm food. Yet here it was, healthy and obviously happy to see them.

"Isn't it wonderful?" Evelyn cooed, giving Blaze a warm hug. Some of her fondest memories were of snuggling with him in front of the fireplace on many a cold winter's night when he was a cub.

"Too bad Zach isn't here," Nate said, sliding the knife into its sheath.

"Won't Ma be shocked?"

"To put it mildly," Nate answered. Winona never had liked the notion of taming wild animals. "Wild things are supposed to *be* wild," she maintained. Having a dog was one thing. A wolf's place was in the forest, not in front of a hearth.

Evelyn stepped back and clutched at her throat. "Oh my gosh, Pa! I almost shot him! I almost killed sweet Blaze!"

"He was lucky," Nate said, thinking of how close he had come to burying his knife. "Let's hope your brother gets back before Blaze takes a notion to go gallivanting off again."

From the end of the lake rose frantic shouts. "Evelyn! Evelyn! Where are you?"

"We're over here, Ma!" Evelyn responded, and tittered. "Come have a look-see! You won't believe who's here!"

Winona had heard a faint scream, then a gunshot. She had been out of her chair and out the door before the shot faded, her Hawken in her hands. Down the trail she had raced, so afraid for her daughter she could barely breathe. Now, hearing Evelyn reply, she felt some of the fear subside. The rest was replaced by resentment when she ran out of the woods onto the shore and spied the cause of all the ruckus bouncing up and down between her husband and her child as they walked toward her. "It cannot be! Him?"

"Him," Nate said, and chuckled. His wife rarely displayed anger, so to see her fit to kick the wolf was highly entertaining.

Evelyn threw an arm around her four-footed friend's furry neck. "Aren't you glad to see him again, Ma? Doesn't it make you want to cry for joy?"

"I could cry, yes," Winona said drily. It wasn't that she disliked Blaze. The wolf had saved her life once, and she would be forever grateful. But she never felt comfortable having it around, especially having it in the cabin.

Her feelings stemmed from her childhood, from that awful winter when heavy snow had been packed deep, half as high as the lodges, and there had been so little to eat that many of her people had perished. In the dead of night she had been awakened by terrible screams, shrill whinnies and shouts. Her father had rushed off. Her mother had comforted a frightened sister.

Winona had wandered outside, and there beheld a scene from her worst nightmare. A pack of hungry wolves had crept into the village, after the horses. Several of the latter were down, the wolves biting at them, heedless of the warriors who so desperately sought to stop the slaughter.

One horse was her own. A pony, a dun her grandfather had given her. Four starving wolves ripped at its belly and neck, tearing off large strips of skin and flesh. Her father was trying to save his own warhorse. There was no one to help her horse.

Winona grabbed a stick from the pile kept handy for the fire, and rushed to the pony's rescue. She swatted and hollered, but the wolves were too hungry to be afraid.

Her pony fought bravely, its hooves knocking wolves away again and again. But it was one against four. And once the wolves had the horse hamstrung, the end was inevitable.

Tears streamed down her cheeks, tears that froze before they reached her chin, as Winona stood and watched her sweet horse being devoured alive. She wept and wept and wept. And wept some more. Her mother found her, whisked her inside, and tried to soothe her. But Winona had not been able to eat or sleep for several days. She had loved that pony. And ever since, she had not been very fond of wolves. Not fond at all.

"Can Blaze sleep with me tonight, Ma, since Zach is gone?" Evelyn was asking. "Please! Oh, please!"

"Maybe he will not want to be indoors," Winona said hopefully.

"Oh, he will! He always loves to curl up by the fire with me. It will be so much fun!"

Winona could think of another word to describe it. She caught her husband smirking, and wagged a finger at him. "Not one peep out of you."

"Yes, dearest." Nate had learned long ago that when a woman was in one of *those* moods, it was best to walk and talk softly until the storm passed. Or better yet, move away. He racked his brain for an excuse to leave for a while.

"Pa's right," Evelyn declared. "It's a shame Zach isn't here. He'd love to see his old friend again."

"Your brother should be back soon," Winona said. Seldom was Stalking Coyote gone more than a week, even on an elk hunt. "He's probably on his way home even as we speak."

"I hope so," Evelyn remarked, then clasped a hand over her mouth. What had she just said? She should wash her mouth out with soap!

Nate gazed off across the stark peaks. He prayed his son was all right. Granted, Shoshone boys were allowed to hunt on their own when they were as young as ten or twelve, and Zach was almost eighteen. But his heart still jumped into his throat every time Zach rode off. Perils were many in the wilderness. He never knew if he was watching his son ride off for the last time.

"Well, until Zach gets back, Blaze is all mine," Evelyn declared. "I can't wait to see if he remembers how to fetch."

Winona sighed. "I can't wait to see if he remembers that he must not lift his leg indoors."

Nate chortled, but his mind was still on Zachary. *Where are you, son?* he wondered. *Wherever it is, I hope you are well.*

At that exact instant, Zachary King was twisting to one side and flinging himself toward the ground. The butcher knife streaked past his chest and imbedded itself in the earth.

Louisa May Clark was on her feet in a bound. She ran toward her pistols. The Shoshone—or whatever he was— would undoubtedly shoot her before she could lay a finger on them. But she would rather die fighting than be a captive in his village for the rest of her life.

Zach realized what she was up to. Pushing onto his hands and knees, he coiled, then leaped, tackling her about the shins. He did not want to hurt her, but she had no such compunctions. As she toppled, her fists rained on his head and shoulders.

"Let go! Let go of me, consarn it!" Louisa tugged and wrenched, but her legs were in a grip of iron. Her flintlocks lay a few feet away. If only she could reach them! She clawed at Stalking Coyote's eyes, but raked his cheek instead.

"Calm down, damn you!" Zach railed. Holding onto her was like trying to hold onto a wildcat. She was slight of build, but wiry and strong. It didn't help that her clothes were so baggy. Trying to get a firm grip was akin to gripping a sheet that billowed in the wind. He winced when her nails raked him, blood seeping from the furrows. "Will you listen to me?"

Lou was beyond listening. She would kill him or he would kill her. She did not care which. Deep down, she secretly hoped he would get the upper hand. That there would come an end to her torment, an end to the horrible misery her broken heart could no longer bear.

Zach had both arms around her waist, and was clawing higher to pin her arms. She resisted tooth and nail, going so far as to sink her teeth into his forearm. Yowling like a stricken cub, he jerked his arm away and felt searing pain. "Simmer down!" he pleaded.

Louisa attempted to knee him in the groin but missed, her knee grazing off his inner thigh. Suddenly he flipped onto his side, swinging her with him, and slammed her onto her back. "No!" she cried, but he was not to be denied. Scrambling atop her, he pressed her arms flat while pinning her legs with his own. "Let me go!"

They were face to face, chest to chest. Zach was flushed and breathing heavily, only partly from the exertion. "You're safe with me!" he exclaimed. "I'd never hurt you!"

"I won't be made a prisoner in any village—" Lou began.

"That was a joke!"

"What?"

"I wasn't serious. Honest. I thought it would make you laugh."

Louisa blinked. "Are you insane?"

"Not that I know of."

"You're holding someone at gunpoint and you *joke* about dragging them off against their will to God knows where?"

Zach laughed, but even to him it sounded as empty as a hollow gourd. "I live with my folks east of here a ways. Me and my sister."

Louisa became very aware of the warmth of his body. Of his warm breath on her cheek. And of his eyes, his fascinating eyes, so deep that looking into them was the same as gazing into a bottomless pool. She shifted to relieve a cramp, her chest rubbing against him in a manner that made her all tingly inside, startling her to her core.

Zach showed as many teeth as a raccoon that had just

caught a crayfish to prove he was sincere, to demonstrate he was not her enemy. Her blue eyes mesmerized him. They shimmered, like the surface of the lake near the cabin. They were the loveliest eyes he had ever seen. It was bewildering. What was wrong with him that he should find a white girl attractive? He tried to speak, but his throat seemed to be clogged with sand. After coughing several times, he offered, "If you promise to behave, I'll let you go."

Louisa was in a quandary. She did not know what to do. She would like to take Stalking Coyote at his word, but dare she trust him? "Will you give my guns back?"

Zach hesitated, weighing his welfare against how she would likely take a refusal. "Only if you give me your word that you won't shoot me."

"What makes you think I'll keep it if I do?"

"I'll just have to trust you," Zach said earnestly. He was, in effect, putting his life in her hands. Maybe he *was* insane.

"You'd do that?" Louisa said, touched by the gesture but still unsure. He had to have an ulterior motive. For the life of her, though, she could not guess what it might be.

"Do we have a deal?" Zach was growing uncomfortable. Her nearness was doing things to his body, making his skin itch and sparking twitches and stirring below his waist.

"Deal," Lou declared, but she felt a twinge of regret when he rose and lowered his hand to help her up. She promptly strode to her pistols. Once armed, she felt safer. Safe enough that she turned her back to him to deal with the elk morsels, which were singed. Removing the spit from the flames, she wagged it. "Hungry, Stalking Coyote?"

Zach was famished. He had to try four times before he could pry a piece off the stick, the meat was so hot. Blowing on it, he nibbled the edges, and when his lips and tongue could stand the heart, he bit into the chunk with relish. "Thank you," he said with his mouth crammed full.

"No need to be grateful. It's your elk." Lou selected a piece for herself. For a while neither of them spoke. She, mainly because she felt uncomfortable. Although she could not say why.

Zach broke the silence. It was odd, but he was intensely curious to learn more about her. "Is Lou your real name? Or were you trying to pass yourself off as a boy?"

"Both," Lou admitted, and revealed her full name. "The ruse is for my own benefit. What do you think would happen if the trappers in these parts learned I was female?"

"You would be up to your neck in suitors." Zach had seen how white men pined for feminine company, particularly the company of their own kind. But white women were as rare as gold west of the Mississippi. So the mountaineers took Indian wives, or else bartered for the privilege of having a maiden live with them a spell.

"Suitors I can do without," Lou said. "I'm too young to be thinking of marriage or courting and such." She quickly added, "Unless I meet the right person, that is. Someone I think highly of." He glanced at her, and she applied her teeth to the meat. What made her say a thing like that? The Shoshone was liable to think she meant him.

Zach bit into another piece to keep from asking the question her comment spurred. What did he care what it took for her to think highly of someone? She was nothing to him. Just another helpless white. Circumstances had thrown them together, and they would soon part. That was it.

"So what's next?" Louisa bluntly asked.

"Tomorrow I'll head home. You can tag along. My mother will take real good care of you. And my father will set to it that you get to wherever you want to go."

Louisa thought of her promise to her pa that she would

look Nate King up. Maybe she should accept Stalking Coyote's offer instead. If only she could be convinced that trusting him was in her best interests!

Zach stuffed the last of the morsel in. "Darn it all. I plumb forgot." He turned to the horses.

Lou was alarmed. "Where are you going?"

"The elk," Zach said. "If I don't butcher it now, there won't hardly be any of it left by morning."

"But it will be pitch dark in less than an hour."

"Then I'll have to work fast." Zach forked leather, nudged to the sorrel to the packhorses, and snagged the lead rope. He saw Louisa's features crease, and he smiled. "I'm not about to run off on you, if that's what you're afraid of."

"I know you wouldn't abandon me," Louisa said. Yet she knew no such thing. So how could she make such an absurd claim? She marched toward the log. "Give me a minute. I'll saddle up. I can help."

Zach immediately responded. "I don't want to put you to any trouble on my account."

Then he shook his head at their antics. A short while ago they had been tearing at each other like cats and dogs. Now they were being polite as could be. Why? He reined the sorrel around and gazed toward the ridge. Even at that distance and in the gathering twilight, the enormous shape climbing toward the crest was impossible to miss. "Look!" he shouted, and slapped his heels against the sorrel.

"What's the matter?" Louisa called out.

"The ridge! Hurry, or it'll drag the carcass off!"

She looked, and gasped. Stalking Coyote was galloping off to stop the one creature her pa had told her must be avoided at all costs.

It was a grizzly.

Chapter Seven

Zachary King had no idea what he was going to do when he reached the ridge. He only knew that he was not going to let the grizzly devour the elk. It was *his* elk. He had spent days tracking it. All that effort was not going to be for naught. Not if he could help it.

Zach let go of the lead rope so he could ride faster. The pack animals would not stray far. Neither was ornery enough. Angling to the left, he came up on the ridge in the same way he had before. The bear had disappeared over the crest. Zach slowed when he gained the base of the slope, and rose in the stirrups. Trees and boulders concealed the spot where the elk lay.

He was taking a godawful chance. His pa had warned him how nasty-tempered grizzlies were. How ferocious the massive brutes were when riled. And how no one could predict how they would react in any given situation because no two silvertips ever reacted the same.

Ever since Zach was a toddler, everyone had been telling him that his father was the greatest killer of grizzlies who ever lived. Zach had pestered his father to learn exactly how many he had slain. But Nate could never remember, or so he claimed.

Zach suspected his father was just too humble to ever boast of his deeds. So Zach had asked Shakespeare McNair. His "uncle" had pegged the total at seven, but allowed as how he "might have missed a few since I'm getting long in the tooth and my memory isn't what it used to be." This from the man who could quote the works of William Shakespeare. Any play. Any sonnet. Anytime.

Zach reined toward a more open part of the slope in case the silvertip rushed him. He climbed slowly, well aware the bear would hear him coming long before he saw it. But it just couldn't be helped.

Gathering twilight compounded the problem. The sun had not yet set, but had dropped below sawtooth peaks to the west, producing the effect of sunset. Lengthening shadows shrouded the undergrowth.

The bear could sneak up on Zach, could be right on top of him, before Zach realized it. For their size, grizzlies were incredibly quick. Over short distances anyway. They could run down a man, even a horse, and disembowel either with a single swipe of their ponderous paws. But while they possessed great strength, they lacked stamina. They tired easily, and would give up the chase if they did not catch their quarry swiftly.

Zach wedged the Hawken to his shoulder. It was powerful enough to bring down a silvertip with one shot if that shot hit a vital organ. A very big if.

A loud snort from above confirmed the grizzly was up there. Zach slanted to where the slope was not quite as steep, and went higher. Suddenly the sorrel caught the bear's scent and shied. Zach firmed his grip on the reins. They went on, the sorrel's ears pricked, its nostrils wide.

A brown hump appeared, bobbing up and down. Zach rose in the stirrups again, and could see the grizzly's shoulders and part of its hindquarters. The monster was tearing into the elk, intent on its feast and nothing else.

Zach moved closer, and the sorrel nickered nervously. Zach tensed, but the silvertip was making so much noise it didn't hear. Soon he was near enough to observe its enormous jaws shear into the elk's soft flesh with the ease of a hot knife shearing into butter. Bone crunched and splintered.

The sorrel's front hoof struck some loose rocks, which clattered down the slope. Grunting, the silvertip stopped eating and reared onto its hind legs. It was gigantic. Eight feet high, possibly more. Dark eyes fixed on horse and rider, and it vented a thunderous growl.

Zach reined up. Was the bear warning them to leave? Or was the growl born of anger at being intruded up on, and was the brute about to attack? When it did not move, Zach waved an arm and yelled, "Shoo! That's my meat, damn your hide!"

Another growl was the grizzly's response. It shifted, tilting its nose upward, and sniffed loudly.

Zach slipped a hand to a pistol. A shot might drive it off. If not, if it had the opposite effect, he would wheel the sorrel and ride like the wind, counting on the slope to lend him the extra speed needed to elude the heavier, clumsier bruin. He pulled the flintlock from under his belt, pointed it at the ground, and rested his thumb on the hammer.

The silvertip dropped onto all fours. Zach feared the worst, but the bear turned and shuffled toward the top of the ridge, apparently unwilling to contest ownership of the carcass. Something a hungry bear would never do. So it must have eaten recently, fortunately for Zach.

He smiled broadly. He had saved the meat without having to tangle with the bear. And he had a fine story he could tell when next he visited the Shoshones. How he had made a mighty grizzly back down. He would be the envy of the other boys his age.

Just then, unexpectedly, Louisa May Clark trotted over the crest.

"No! Go back!" Nate bawled.

The bear stopped and raised its huge head in alarm at being caught between the two of them. To its way of thinking, they were trying to trap him. So it reacted as would any cornered animal. It roared and went after the girl.

Louisa had saddled Fancy as rapidly as she could. But Stalking Coyote had been out of sight by the time she trotted from the stand. She had been surprised to find the packhorses grazing unattended, and had taken the time to round them up and tie them to convenient trees. Then she had sped toward the ridge. Anxious over Stalking Coyote's safety, she had gone up the near side instead of around to the east.

Lou had gone slowly once she reached the slope. She had planned to take her sweet time and peek over the top without showing herself. But when she'd heard Stalking Coyote yell, and had not quite made out what he said, she'd leaped to the conclusion he was in danger. Up the slope she'd flown, to trot on over the crest and discover the grizzly not twenty feet below. Zach was much lower, and safe. She hiked an arm to wave to him.

The bear charged.

Louisa cut the reins and fled. She did not know how fast grizzlies were, but she had every confidence Fancy could outrun it. Fancy could outrun anything. The mare streaked on down the ridge at a reckless rate, dirt and rocks cascading out from under her hooves.

A backward glance showed the bear had just reached the top. Lou grinned and lashed the reins. Fancy would leave the critter in the dust. She avoided boulders, a log, and several trees, winding through them as skillfully as a Comanche.

Zachary King, meanwhile, was lashing his own mount upward. In his mind's eye he saw the silvertip swat the girl from her saddle and rend her limb from limb. Frantic, he galloped over the top, and was elated to behold Louisa alive and pulling well ahead of the grizzly. He yipped for joy, and waved.

Lou heard the cry. Twisting, she smiled and straightened to return the gesture, to show she was safe. For several seconds her gaze lingered on Stalking Coyote. And so it was that she failed to spot an obstacle directly below. A deadfall, downed trees all jumbled together on top of one another. Only when Fancy whinnied did she look. She hauled on the reins, but there was no avoiding it.

The mare launched herself into the air. In a graceful arc Fancy sailed up and over. Or tried to. The piled trees were too high. Fancy's front legs cleared them, but not her rear legs. A sharp *crack,* a jarring lurch, and the mare cartwheeled.

Louisa clutched at the saddle as the world spun upside down. In a twinkling she was flying; she had been thrown clear. Tumbling end over end, she felt a severe pain in her side, another in her leg. Her shoulder smashed onto the ground, and she rolled. It sounded as if an avalanche cascaded down the slope in her wake. But it was something else, as she learned when she slid to a painful stop.

Dust clogged her nose, her mouth. Louisa sputtered and coughed and tried to sit up, but a tremendous weight on her lower legs held her down. She swatted at the roiling dust, then groped lower. Her hand brushed the saddle. She heard the mare nicker.

''Fancy?'' Louisa said between coughs. Bending, she saw the horse struggling to rise. Struggling weakly. Blood oozed from a nostril, and a ragged gash marred the mare's shoulder. ''Please, no!''

Fancy was more than a horse. She was Louisa's friend. The only friend Louisa had had during those long months spent trapping with her father. Every day without fail, she had taken Fancy for a ride, talking to the mare as she would to a boon companion. Every evening without exception, she had brushed the mare's mane and tail and fed Fancy handfuls of sweet grass.

Fancy mustn't be hurt! Louisa pushed and prodded, but she could not extricate herself. Placing her elbows flat, she heaved backward. Her legs moved an inch, if that. She braced to try again. Then went as rigid as a board.

Beyond Fancy an enormous hulking form had materialized. A nightmare made real. The grizzly had skirted the deadfall.

"Oh, God!" Louisa exclaimed. She erupted in a frenzy, doing everything and anything she could think of to free herself, to no avail. The mare was just too heavy. Helpless, trapped, she watched, aghast, as the shaggy behemoth lumbered to a halt a few yards away. Eyes as black as the pits of Hades burned into hers, then settled on the mare.

At that same moment, on top of the ridge, Zach smacked his Hawken against the sorrel and hurtled down the slope to the girl's aid. His heart had seemed to stop when her horse had spilled. He'd lost sight of her, his view blocked by the deadfall, but he'd seen the bear run faster and had guessed its intent.

Zach's chest was constricted; his temples pounded. It would take him twenty to thirty seconds to reach them. An eternity. More than long enough for the silvertip to reduce Louisa to a quivering mass of pulped flesh. *Please, no!* he prayed, without realizing he was doing so.

Fancy neighed shrilly in abject fright. Louisa kept pushing against the saddle, but it was like trying to move a five-ton boulder. The grizzly moved closer, its gigantic head swinging from side to side. Lou grabbed for both pistols, finding to her dismay that one was gone. Leveling the other, she aimed at the center of the bear's forehead.

"Leave us be!" Louisa shrieked. But she might as well have been throwing wads of paper. The silvertip paid no more attention to her than it would to the buzzing of a bee. She had to shoot, even if she only wounded it and incited it into a rage. She had no choice.

The hammer was a blur. The flintlock hissed like a

snake, spewed smoke and flame—and that was it. "A misfire!" she railed, grasping her powder horn. A minute was all she needed! In a minute she could reload. She could save Fancy and herself. But she did not have that minute. She did not have ten seconds.

The bear had caught the scent of pulsing blood, and was sniffing like a hound on a fresh trail. A paw the size of Louisa's head flicked out. Claws as thick as her thumbs sheared into Fancy's side, and the mare squealed, a squeal remarkably like a woman's.

Zach King thought it was Louisa. He was going so fast that a misstep would result in grave injury or much worse, but he prodded the sorrel to go even faster. He did not care what happened to him. Saving the girl was all that counted. Saving her at all costs.

Again a paw ripped into Fancy. Louisa was beside herself with mingled fury and fear. Her fingers flying, she continued to reload. The silvertip swung a third time, and crimson spray spewed every which way. Somehow a couple of drops got into Louisa's mouth. She tasted warm, salty liquid, and nearly gagged.

Fancy was thrashing and kicking, wheezing and spitting blood. And bleeding, bleeding heavily from deep punctures that had partially exposed several ribs. The mare made a valiant effort to stand, and succeeded in getting her legs under her. But when she rose onto her knees, the grizzly snarled and struck, razor claws slashing into her neck. A red torrent gushed.

Louisa had stopped reloading to scramble backward again. Fancy had risen just enough to remove most of the pressure on Louisa's legs. Spotting a sapling, Louisa wrapped both forearms around it for leverage. Her shoulders strained to their utmost. Much too slowly, she pulled herself toward the tree. Fancy whinnied again. The bear roared. Something wet and slippery slapped against Louisa's cheek, then plopped to the grass. It was a strip of flesh.

Suddenly Louisa's legs were free. She rolled onto her

back, then sat up and looked to see how Fancy was faring. Fancy was dead. Head limp, neck skewed at an unnatural angle, the mare had succumbed.

The silvertip's front paws were on Fancy's chest, and the bear was staring at Louisa now. She froze. She did not breathe. Not even when the grizzly's head dipped low enough for saliva dribbling from its lower jaw to fall onto her face. Its fetid breath fanned her. It sniffed some more.

Louisa recalled a trapper telling her that bears lived by their sense of smell. Their eyesight was supposedly poor, their hearing no better than average. Their sense of smell, though, was extraordinary; they could detect a whiff of prey hundreds of yards away. They were, as the grizzled old trapper had phrased it, "these awful eatin' machines attached to the best noses this side of a bloodhound."

The trapper had shared an interesting notion. Whenever he found bear sign in an area he was trapping, he always sprinkled dirt on his buckskins and rubbed it all over his skin and hair. "Dirt is the one thing those demons won't eat," he had explained, "so I figure if I smell like dirt, they'll leave me be."

It was too late for Louisa to try the same ruse. She resisted an urge to bolt. The bear's head hovered inches above hers, and it was still inhaling deeply. Maybe it would ignore her. Maybe it would turn to the mare and she could sneak off.

The grizzly started to turn. It placed one paw on the ground, and was lowering its mouth to Fancy, when it unexpectedly stood stock still and stared right at Louisa. She could not imagine why. She had not moved. Or so she assumed until she blinked for a second time. And the moment she did, the silvertip emitted a thunderous roar and attacked.

Louisa blindly scrambled backwards. A blow that would have separated her head from her body instead reduced the sapling to slivers. She pumped her limbs in a whirlwind of desperation, half crawling, half sliding out of the bear's reach. But not for long. The silvertip was up and over Fancy in a nimble-footed bound. It tramped toward her, in no particular hurry. Why should it be? It had her dead to rights and knew it.

Pushing to her feet, Lousia sprinted to the left, toward an open space. She had never run faster in her life, but she was molasses compared to her pursuer. A paw clipped her on the shoulder. The impact smashed her like a broken doll to the earth. Dazed and weak, she craned her neck to look back.

The silvertip was almost on top of her. With deliberate, weighty tread, it stalked closer, steadily closer, seeming to fill half the sky.

Louisa knew she was a goner. She had thought she would be happy when her time came, but she wasn't. Now she would pass on to the other side of the veil and rejoin her folks, but Lord help her, she did not want to. Not yet. She regretted not being able to tell Stalking Coyote good-bye.

"NOOOoooooooo!"

The cry was torn from Zach King's throat by emotions he did not fully understand. He had the Hawken flush with his shoulder, and when the silvertip swung toward him, he fired.

The ball penetrated between the brute's forelegs. It missed the heart and the lungs, but it distracted the grizzly from the girl. Slavering and yowling, the grizzly reared as it had done earlier.

Zach switched the reins to the same hand that held his rifle so he could flourish a pistol. The .55-caliber smooth-bore could drop most any animal at close enough range. He tried to take a steady bead, but the sorrel's rolling gait caused the muzzle to rise and fall. He squeezed the trigger anyway, then hunched forward, not letting the sorrel break stride.

Louisa thought she must be mistaken. It did not appear as if Stalking Coyote were going to stop. A collision would be as harmful to him and the horse as the bear. Stupefied, she saw her would-be rescuer set his jaw in grim determination, saw him flick the reins, saw the fear in the sorrel's eyes.

The horse slammed into the grizzly with the force of a battering ram, and the bear tottered backward. Ungainly when erect, it could not keep its footing and toppled, landing in brush that buckled under its immense frame.

Zach's mount nearly did likewise. Slipping and sliding, it careened into a tree, almost unhorsing him. They slid another thirty feet before coming to a halt in a shower of dirt and dust. Zach whipped out his other pistol, then brought the sorrel around to confront the silvertip again. "Run!" he shouted at the girl, bewildered when she did not listen.

Louisa couldn't run. She couldn't stand. Her legs were mush, her mind little better. Her shoulder had not been torn open, but it throbbed with agony. "I can't!" she replied. "Save yourself!"

The bear had risen on all fours, and glared balefully. Zach kneed the sorrel toward Louisa, hoping he could sweep her up behind him and get out of there while the monster was collecting its wits. If it had wits to collect.

Snarling viciously, the silvertip exploded out of the crushed brush. "Stand up!" Zach bellowed. Louisa tried, but her legs refused to cooperate. She did thrust her arm overhead so he could grab it on the fly.

Zach was not about to risk dislocating her shoulder or breaking a bone. He slowed, bending down, his arm curled. Right away he realized Louisa was too low to the ground for him to catch hold of her. So he straightened and reined up, overshooting her by a few yards. Vaulting to the ground, he raced over, scooped Louisa up, and turned.

The sorrel was so close, yet so far. Zach sprang toward it and grasped at the saddle. As his hand found purchase, the horse shied. Not from him, but from the silvertip, which would be upon them in another few moments. Zach lost his hold and stumbled to his knees, holding the girl close.

David Thompson

Louisa saw the slavering bear. "Save yourself!" she repeated. Burdened by her, she knew, Stalking Coyote could never escape. "Please!"

The very idea that he would abandon someone in a crisis went against Zach's grain. It was contrary to everything his pa had taught him, everything Uncle Shakespeare believed, and the ideals by which Shoshone warriors were expected to live. "Never! If we die, we die together!"

It was the bravest thing Louisa had ever heard. She threw her arms around his neck, pressed her cheek to his, and wished they had been able to get to know one another a whole lot better. He aroused sensations in her no one ever had. Feelings that excited and scared her. Feelings she would never feel again, because in a few seconds both of them would be dead.

The grizzly's horrid maw yawned wide. Yet it was not them the bear was after. It veered toward the sorrel—and was met by clubbing hooves. Instead of fleeing, the horse fought back. Bucking its rear legs furiously, the sorrel kicked the silvertip again and again and again. The *thud-thud-thud* of hooves on bone was like the pounding of a blacksmith's hammer on an anvil. Three times the grizzly sought to grapple with its prey, and each time those flashing mallets drove it back.

Blood poured from a gash over the beast's left eye. There was a ghastly furrow below the right ear. And then a hoof crunched against teeth, and two fell out.

The griz had had enough. Growling in a fit of foul temper, it whirled with unbelievable agility and loped to the south, shaking its squat head every so often as if to clear it. Just before entering the forest, it halted and looked back. With a final snarl of defiance, the lord of the Rockies was gone.

"Thank God!" Louisa breathed, clinging to the one who had risked his life for hers. Mere days ago she would never have let herself be so close to a boy. But this felt natural. It felt right. "And thank you, Stalking Coyote.

98

You almost got yourself killed on my account. I'll never forget what you did.''

"Thank my horse," Zach said. New emotions roiled within him. He felt grateful, awkward, happy, upset. Yet how could he feel all of them at the same time? It was preposterous.

The sorrel pranced back and forth, snorting and kicking as if it were eager to tear into the silvertip again.

Seconds dragged past. Zach was in no hurry to stand, or to let go of Louisa. He savored the interlude, trying to recollect the last time he had felt so . . . pleasant . . . in the presence of a female. It had been six years ago, when he had been captured by the Blackfeet and befriended by a Blackfoot maiden. She had been special, just like Louisa Clark.

What was he thinking? What had gotten into him? This was a white girl, a member of the very race that despised him the most. In the eyes of her people he was a "breed." The same as saying he was "worthless." Hadn't he vowed that he wanted nothing to do with whites? Weren't they all bigots?

Well, not *all*. His father wasn't. Uncle Shakespeare wasn't. Scott Kendall wasn't. And there were others who treated him with the respect every person was due no matter what their skin color might be.

Coughing, Zach looked down at Louisa. She was looking up at him. Their eyes met, and locked. Zach did not say anything, afraid of breaking the spell.

For her part, Louisa was as content as content could be. Her harrowing escapade was forgotten. Being adrift in a sea of wilderness was forgotten. She would never forget her father's gruesome death, but at the moment, for the first time since it happened, it did not weigh heavily on her mind. Happiness had claimed her.

The sorrel shattered their special moment by nudging Zach hard enough to make him pitch forward. To avoid falling on top of Louisa, he had to release her. His outflung hands stopped him from landing on his stomach, and he started to rise in anger. Merry laughter brought him up short.

Louisa thought his expression was comical. He looked as if he was set to finish the job the silvertip had started. Once she started laughing, she couldn't stop. She went on and on, laughing until it hurt, laughing until tears glistened on her cheeks and she could not laugh any more.

Zach joined in, pleased she was so happy, but sensing there was more to it than what the sorrel had done. When she eventually stopped, he helped her stand. "I'll take you back to camp, then tend to the elk."

"Nonsense. I'm fine," Louisa said. A barefaced lie. Her shoulder was next to useless. "It wouldn't be fair for you to do all the work."

Zach disagreed, but he did not argue. He did insist she stay on the sorrel while he stripped the saddle and blanket off the dead mare. "From here on out you can ride one of the packhorses."

Louisa avoided staring at Fancy. Her friend was gone, and that was that. To get emotional over it would be childish. Yet she was glad when Zach deposited her saddle on a boulder, to be retrieved later, and they rode on over the crest to examine the elk's carcass. A few more moments and she would have burst into tears.

The silvertip had taken giant bites out of the elk. A whole haunch was nearly gone. Enough remained, though, to last the King family for a month, so Zach's hunt had not been wasted. They carved it up, working side by side until long after the sun had relinquished the heavens to twinkling stars.

Blood and gore caked Louisa up to her elbows, but she did not mind. Occasionally, while they worked, her arm brushed Stalking Coyote's, and she minded that even less. Which both puzzled and amused her. Just yesterday she'd hated all Indians. Now here she was, supremely happy to be in the company of one. Was she fickle, as her pa always claimed women were? Could a person change their whole outlook in so short a time?

Zach wiped his hands on a piece of elk hide. It was time to fetch the packhorses. Another hour and they would be done. Tomorrow, they would dry the meat. By the day after, they could leave. He wondered how his folks would react to his new friend. Suddenly, a noise from down the slope made that the least of his worries. "The bear."

Louisa was slicing meat off a hipbone. It was the last of the elk untouched by the grizzly. She thought of taking a dip in the stream in the morning. To wash off the blood, nothing more. "What about him?" she absently asked.

"He's come back."

Chapter Eight

Evelyn King was as happy as a squirrel with a big old pine cone to chew. Lying on a bearskin rug in front of the fireplace, she hugged Blaze, nuzzling his neck with her chin. "I love you so much," she cooed, and was rewarded with a wet tongue on the tip of her nose. She giggled, then rubbed behind his ears. "I hope you never go away again."

Seated in a rocking chair, Winona glanced up from her sewing and frowned. Her daughter was in for a disappointment. The wolf would not stay long. It never did anymore. That it came at all never ceased to amaze her. "Do not become too attached to him," she cautioned.

"I already am, Ma." Evelyn kissed Blaze on the forehead. "Don't you know that by now?"

Nate King was at the table, cleaning his pistols and rifles. "Just remember he's a wild animal, little one," he said. "We can never truly tame him."

"He'd never hurt any of us, Pa. Not ever."

She had misunderstood, so Nate set her straight. "He

likes us, yes, but his heart is in the deep woods, in the wild places his kind have roamed since the dawn of time. He likes his freedom. So one day soon he'll just disappear again.''

Winona bent to her sewing, amused at how different men and women were. She had tried to spare her daughter's feelings by not coming right out and saying it. But not Nate. Men were more direct about things; women had more compassion. Women were always less inclined to hurt another person.

Winona often wondered why the two sexes were so unlike. The Great Mystery—or God, as her husband called that which was above all else—had to have done it for a reason. Nothing in life *ever* happened without a reason. But it seemed to her that relations would be better all around if women and men shared more traits in common. They would be less at odds. There would be less bickering, less fighting.

She remembered how shocked she had been their first year of married life. Here she'd thought she had known all there was to know about men. She had a father, did she not? And male cousins? She had lived among men all her life. So she could be excused for believing she had learned all there was to learn about their stubborn, strutting ways.

How wrong she had been! Only a woman who had lived with a man for any length of time could appreciate how little unmarried women truly knew. All the strange things men did! So many quirks, it would take hours to detail them.

Her dearly beloved was a prime example. Nate had to have his clothes folded in half, no other way. His belongings must always be arranged in a certain order. When it came to neatness, he was fanatical, insisting the cabin be spotlessly clean. And where food was concerned, he was worse. His eggs had to be just so. His toast must never be too crispy. His meat must always be cooked rare. He could not abide loud noises when he was reading. And so on and so on. Enough to drive a woman to drink.

Winona looked at him and wondered if he thought the same about her. If he was nettled by her quirks. But no, that could not be. She had no quirks. She was too sensible. The normal one.

Evelyn had not said anything for a while. Now she rolled onto her side, propped her cheek in a hand, and asked, "When I get older, can I marry any man I want?"

Nate had started to shove the ramrod into the Hawken, and missed. "You're a little young to be worrying about things like that, aren't you?"

"I'll be nine my next birthday. Not much younger than Red Fawn."

Winona leaned back. So that was it. During their last visit to her people, they had learned that Red Fawn, the daughter of a close friend, had been promised to the son of a prominent warrior. Both were much too young to move into a lodge together anytime soon; the marriage would not take place until they came of age. She reminded Evelyn of that now.

"Oh, I know, Ma. But that's not my point. Will Pa and you let me marry whoever I want? Or will you make me marry someone I might not care for?"

Nate was upset his own flesh and blood would even think he could do such a thing. "I'd never force you to do anything against your will, little one."

Evelyn snickered. "You make me do the dishes. And make my bed. And clean up all the time. And I have to take turns with Zach feeding the horses."

"Chores are different."

Winona was pondering her daughter's question. Pondering what might be the underlying cause. "Is Red Fawn unhappy that she must marry Tall Elk one day?" she asked Evelyn.

"Yes. She likes another boy better. She asked her father not to do it, but he told her the marriage would be good for her and for their family. Tall Elk's pa has many horses."

Which was another way of saying that, by Indian standards, Tall Elk's father was wealthy. Winona could not fault Red Fawn's father for wanting to improve the family's lot in life, as her husband would say. Frequently, daughters were pledged to mates they had never met.

Nate sighed. He did not approve of the practice and never would. A girl should have the right to choose. Many decades ago arranged marriages had been common over in Europe, but in recent years the attitude had changed. Women were being granted more freedoms than ever before, although not nearly enough, in his estimation.

If asked, he would admit his own attitude had undergone a great change since his younger days, largely due to Shakespeare. Before he came West he had never given the status of women much thought. They were *there*. They had babies. They were fine mothers. What else counted?

Then one day some missionaries arrived at the annual Rendezvous. Marcus Whitman was the leader of that group, and at Whitman's side was his remarkable wife, Narcissa. She befriended Winona, and two spent much time together.

Nate and Shakespeare had been watching them converse when Nate happened to remark, "That Narcissa is some woman. Never lets anything fluster her. Not even Joe Meek." Meek was a notorious braggart who took delight in intimidating others.

Shakespeare laughed. "Yes, she's as fine as they come. Forthright. Honest. Upstanding. Too bad she can't vote, isn't it?"

The odd comment perplexed Nate. "What does voting have to do with anything?"

"I would say it has everything to do with everything."

"Speak plain for once. Your tongue could twist a rope into knots all by its lonesome."

"You really think so?" Shakespeare was flattered. "As for voting, it's the measure by which you can judge how free someone is."

"I've lost your trail."

"Follow me, then." Shakespeare made himself comfortable on a stump and took out his pipe. "Do you and I have the right to vote?"

"If we were back in the States, yes, we would. But out here there is no government, so voting isn't important."

"Fie on thee, Horatio. Voting is always important. It separates the citizen from the lazy leech." Shakespeare took a pouch containing tobacco from his possibles bag. "And quit being so literal. In the States you and I can vote, can we not?"

"Of course."

"Can blacks vote?"

"No. Not the slaves. Freeborn blacks can."

"A mere handful." McNair began to fill the bowl. "As a general rule, can blacks vote?"

"No."

"Can children?"

"That's silly. No. They're too young."

"Can women?"

"No."

"Why not? Are they too young?"

"No, of course not, but—"

"Are they slaves?"

"You're being ridiculous. No, women are not slaves."

"Yet we treat them just as if they are. Does that strike you as fair?"

Nate had never thought of it in that context before, and he was troubled. "No, I reckon it doesn't."

"Then there is hope for you yet." Shakespeare chuckled. "But imagine how your own mother must have felt. All those years they were married, all those elections your father proudly took part in, doing his civic duty, and she wasn't allowed to so much as set foot in a polling place. You never questioned the wisdom of that?''

"No," Nate was ashamed to admit.

"Youth no less becomes the light and careless livery that it wears than settled age his sables and his weeds, importing health and graveness," McNair then quoted. "Don't feel bad. I might not have given it any thought either, if not for my first wife. She was as free a spirit as an eagle. And she keenly resented being treated inferior to anyone."

Nate's interest was piqued. "You never mentioned her before. Where is she now?"

"Martha? Dead."

"Oh. I'm sorry."

"Not anywhere near as sorry as I am. I loved her, loved her dearly."

"How did she die, if I may ask?"

Shadows clouded Shakespeare's craggy face. "She upped and left me, son. I'd worshiped the ground she walked on, but I was never quite good enough for her, never quite handsome enough or rich enough. So she took up with a perfect gentleman, or so she thought." McNair spat. "True gentlemen are as rare as hen's teeth, and this one turned out to be as false as politician. His name was Craven. He was a worthless rogue, a lazy scoundrel. He left her alone every night while he caroused with fallen doves."

"He shouldn't have," Nate declared. While he may not have given much thought to the status of women in society, he did firmly believe that no man had the right to mistreat his wife. Not after having witnessed the abuse his mother had endured for so many years.

"My sentiments exactly," Shakespeare said. "But the worst was yet to come. Martha came down sick and he didn't lift a finger to help her. He never sent for a doctor. Nothing."

"She lived, though?"

"In point of fact, she did not. Martha spent a week in the most awful agony, then died. I was at her side, holding her hand, the whole time." The oldest living mountaineer bowed his white-maned head. "I had a physician come, but it was too late. She was too far gone. So I took it on myself to have her buried in the family cemetery. Invited everyone she knew. Even the scum who killed her."

Nate was astounded. "I would have slit his throat."

"We think alike, sweet Horatio," Shakespeare responded. "Because that is exactly what I did. While he was standing there beside her grave, pretending to be grief-stricken, his hat in hand, I walked right up to him, looked him right in the eyes, and cut him from ear to ear. Damn near chopped off the bastard's head."

Nate felt a need to sit down. His expression must have given his thoughts away, for Shakespeare motioned testily.

"Do you condemn me for not letting the wretch live? Should I have played the fool and treated him as if nothing of consequence had occurred?" Shakespeare rubbed his eyes. "Lord help me, I could not. So I did what everyone there secretly wanted to do but could not bring themselves to carry out."

"How much time did you spend in prison?"

"None. I fled."

Insight flooded through Nate like water over a dam. "You headed for the frontier. Beyond the reach of the law."

"Yes, Horatio, I did. So now, at long last, you know the real reason I was one of the first white men to venture west of the Mississippi. I wasn't guided by a grand desire to explore the wilds. I had no hankering to see the Rockies. No, I came West because I did not want to spend the rest of my life behind bars. Or be hung by the neck until I was dead, dead, dead."

Nate had often wondered why his mentor had traveled into the unknown at a time when most whites felt to do so was certain death. "You've never been back?"

"Never."

"What about the rest of your family? They must have missed you terribly."

"They disowned me."

"No! How could they?"

Shakespeare stared at his pipe, then shoved it into his possibles bag. "Didn't feel much liking smoking, anyhow."

"You don't want to talk about it?"

McNair frowned. " 'I did think thee, for two ordinaries, to be a pretty wise fellow. Thou didst make tolerable vent of thy travel.' " Removing his beaver hat, he ran his calloused fingers through his long hair. When next he spoke, his voice was so low Nate could barely hear it. "My father was a minister, son. As spiritual a person as you will ever meet. He was a firm believer in turning the other cheek. But he was not much on forgiveness. Not where his own son was involved."

"He held it against you?"

"He forbade me to ever set foot in his house again. Or to have any contact with my mother or the rest of my siblings." Shakespeare seemed to age another ten years. "I wrote them many times, but he never answered. Mother did once. My sister twice. They both mentioned how no one was allowed to talk about me or even speak my name. My father went so far as to blot it from the front of the family bible, where the record of our family history was kept. In its place, he wrote in large black letters, 'Murderer Most Foul.' "

Nate did not know what to say, so he did not say anything.

"But do you know what, son? To this day I don't regret what I did. I like to think that Martha looked up from her grave and smiled when she saw that vermin bleeding his life away." McNair straightened and mustered a grin. " 'I do profess to be no less than I seem. To serve him truly that will put me in trust. To love him that is honest. To converse with him that is wise and says little. To fear judgment. To fight when I cannot choose, and to eat no fish.' ''

What fish had to do with the whole affair, Nate could not say then, nor could he say now years later. Shaking himself, he gazed at his daughter. ''When the time comes, you can marry whoever you want.''

''Thank you, Pa.''

''Just so long as he's not a rogue and a scoundrel.''

Zachary King fed a broken branch to the fire, then sat back to stare at the sleeping girl across from him. He was mighty tired, too, but he had told her he would keep watch so she could catch up on her rest.

One of the packhorses nickered, and Zach had half a mind to chuck a stone at it. It was the same one that had strayed to the ridge earlier, after it had pulled free of the lead rope. He had mistaken it for the bear.

Louisa had rushed to his side, declaring, ''We'll fight it together!'' When they saw it was the horse, they had laughed, and she had thrown her arms around his neck. Almost immediately she had stopped laughing and stepped back, embarrassed. ''Sorry,'' she had said softly.

Zach had not been, not one whit. He had liked the feel of her skin on his, of her being so close he could feel her heart pound in her chest. Yet it should not be. She was white, through and through. She did not have a drop of Indian blood in her. So *why* was he so attracted to her? He had always taken it for granted that when he felt these kind of feelings for a woman, it would be for an Indian woman. A Shoshone.

He rested his elbows on his knees and his face in his hands. What was happening to him? Why could he not stop thinking of that fleeting embrace? Of earlier, when they had grappled? Of her charming smile? And the adoration in her eyes when she looked at him?

Zach figured it must have something to do with the dreams he had been having for some time now. Dreams of women. Women who did things with him he had never imagined doing. Well, almost never. Sometimes he would awaken after one of these dreams, his whole body hot, and want to run down to the lake and jump in.

Long ago his father had told him there would come a day when he would think as highly of women as he did of his former pet wolf. Zach had laughed. Maybe it happened to other men, but it would *never* happen to him. He was different.

"Maybe I'm not so different after all," he said aloud.

"Different how, Stalking Coyote?"

Zach jerked up, perturbed she had heard him. "I thought you were sound asleep." He did not explain his comment.

Louisa slowly sat and stretched. "I've tried and tried, but I can't doze off for the life of me." Which should not be the case. She was exhausted. She *felt* exhausted. Every muscle, every fiber of her being craved sleep. Yet her mind was racing like a Thoroughbred. She could not stop thinking about *him*. And she had tried. Oh, *how* she had tried. She had scolded herself for being so childish, and sought to convince herself he was nothing special.

But now, admiring his handsome features out of the corner of an eye, Louisa could not deny the truth. He was special. She liked being with him. Liked how he talked and how he moved and how he looked at her sometimes when he thought she would not notice. "How old are you, exactly?" she asked.

"What difference does it make?"

"None," Louisa lied. What if she were wrong and he was younger than she was? "I just wanted something to talk about and it was the first thing that popped into my head."

"I've seen eighteen winters," Zach hedged. His birthday was not for months yet, but it was close enough. "You."

"Sixteen."

"A very mature sixteen."

"Oh? You really think so?"

Zach could not say what he thought. The compliment had gushed out of nowhere. "Sure. The way you handled yourself with that bear showed you're not a little girl."

"Thank you. I sure don't feel like a girl," Louisa agreed, although until that very moment she had never considered herself anything *but*.

Quiet claimed them.

Zach tried to think of something witty or interesting to say, and could not. His mind was as empty as an upended cup. Which had never happened to him before.

Louisa was content to be silent. She admired him on the sly, glad he was not one of those gabby types who could never shut up. Boys like that always set her teeth on edge. But then, she had to remind herself that Stalking Coyote wasn't a boy. He was a man.

The wavering howl of a wolf reminded Louisa of something else. "Are we safe here? Do you reckon that silvertip will come back?"

"He's probably miles off," Zach said to spare her added anxiety. Based on the tales his father imparted, the griz might be watching them at that very second, waiting for them to turn in. A few years ago several trappers had been ripped to bits in their sleep by one. "We're as safe here as anywhere else."

"I hope so."

Zach noted the glance she threw at the benighted woods. "You can bring your blanket around to this side of the fire, if you have a hankering to." The moment the words were out of his mouth, he wanted to punch himself in the teeth for saying them.

Louisa never hesitated. She had spread it out on the other side initially just because it was the proper thing to do. A lady did not sleep close to a man she had just met. But she had no qualms about rolling it up and moving to within a couple of feet of her benefactor. As she spread it out again, she had a thought that scared her. "Are you married, Stalking Coyote?"

Zach snorted. "Whatever gave you that notion? I'm too young to have a wife."

"I've known plenty of men your age who were hitched, and had kids besides," Louisa mentioned.

"I've known a few, too," Zach responded, hoping he had not hurt her feelings. Then it hit him. She had called him a *man*. He sat a little straighter and squared his shoulders. "I bet when you get back to the States, the first thing you'll do is wed some lucky fella."

"There isn't anyone back there who interests me in the least," Louisa said. Then it hit her. He had said that the man who claimed her heart would be *lucky*. She lay on the blanket, closer to him than her father would have deemed fitting.

"A pretty lady like you will be up to elbows in suitors in no time," Zach predicted. "Among the Shoshones, you'd have been spoken for long ago."

Lou recalled the visit her pa and her paid to St. Louis on their trek westward. One night they had gone for a stroll and blundered onto a street of ill repute. Women in tight dresses had lined both sides, beckoning to passersby. Her father had commanded her to avert her eyes and march straight ahead, but she could not resist taking a peek. Those women had a way about them. A way of luring men like a flame lured moths. She wished now that she could be as alluring, that she knew the tricks they did to make themselves so irresistible.

Zach thought of something to say at last. "Tell me about your life."

"It would bore you to death."

"No. Honestly. I'd like to hear it," Zach assured her. The wonder of it was, he was serious.

Louisa humored him. Haltingly at first, she shared details about her childhood. A childhood so ordinary there was not much to share. She had grown up in a small town in Ohio, Grinder's Mill. Until she was five they had lived with her grandparents, her pa's folks. Then her parents had gotten a small place of their own.

David Thompson

Her father worked a number of jobs, and was never satisfied with any. He was always scraping to make ends meet. Always fretting about having enough money to provide a decent life. He would go on and on about how Ma deserved better. How he would like to give her the biggest house and the finest clothes. Her mother would always say that was sweet, but she was happy with his love.

Her pa always wanted to get rich quick. But most of his attempts ended like the time he hooked up with a man from New York who was selling shares in a big company. Her father had forked over most of their savings, only to have the New Yorker disappear. The company, it turned out, did not exist.

Their quest for beaver was but the last in a long line of schemes. And it had cost him more than money. Now her mother and her father had gone to their reward, leaving her all alone in the world.

"Don't you have kin back East?" Zach asked.

"My grandparents have long since died. My ma had a sister, but I wouldn't know where to begin to look for her. She never wanted a thing to do with us." Louisa shivered as a stiff gust from the northwest rustled the trees.

"Cold, are you?" Zach said. He had a spare blanket. But rather than fetch it, he stretched out on his back beside her. "I can keep you warm. If you want." The chill did not bother him. It never did.

Louisa had never wanted anything more. She shyly pressed against his side. Their bodies barely touching, she lowered her cheek to his chest.

Zach was stunned. He had not expected her to do it. Awkwardly, almost fearfully, he draped an arm over her slim shoulder. For a long while he just lay there, dumbfounded by his own boldness. Then he said softly, "Care to hear about my life?"

She did not answer.

"It's not all that exciting either. Unless you count

when the Apaches tried to make wolf meat of us. Or when the Blackfeet took me captive. Or when we went to the Pacific Ocean.'' Zach stopped. She still had not responded. "Louisa?" Looking down, he learned why.

She was sound asleep.

Zachary King squeezed her arm, gently placed his cheek against the top of her head, and smiled at the stars.

Chapter Nine

"Look! He's doing it again, Pa."

"So he is."

Evelyn King had been keeping count. This made the fourth time that morning. "Why is he doing it so much? I never saw him act this way before." It saddened her to see Blaze so upset. Yet there he was, nose to the ground, roving frantically back and forth while whining pitiably.

"I reckon he just misses your brother a lot," Nate responded. His son and the wolf had always enjoyed an exceptional bond. "Blaze knows that Zach must have gone off somewhere, so he's trying to pick up Zach's scent."

Evelyn recalled how great Blaze was at finding people. He could sniff out anyone anywhere. When she and Zach were younger, one of their favorite games had been to play hide-and-seek. One of them would go off and hide, then the other would get the wolf to hunt. Blaze always found them. Always. No matter how far they went. No matter what kind of tricks they tried.

"Blaze is confused because he can't find where your brother's scent leads away from the cabin," Nate mentioned.

Evelyn knew why. "Zach was on the sorrel. So all Blaze smells is the sorrel's scent, huh, Pa?"

"Smart girl." Nate patted the top rail of the corral. "I'm going inside for some coffee. Are you coming?"

"In a bit," Evelyn said. "I'd like to stay out here and play with Blaze a spell. If you don't mind." She remembered how she and Zach had trained Blaze to follow a scent, and wondered if it would still work. Maybe she could help the wolf. Wouldn't Zach be surprised when Blaze came trotting up? She would give anything to see the look on his face.

Nate's Hawken was propped against the corner of the cabin. Grasping it, he strolled to the doorway. The day was warm and pleasant, with birds singing nearby, and a soft breeze was blowing. The kind of day that made him doubly glad he lived in the wilds. "Don't be too long. Your mother wanted some help sewing a dress."

"I know. I'll be along directly," Evelyn promised. As soon as her father had gone in, she rushed to the gate, opened it, and hurried across the pen to the tack shed. On the north side of the cabin was another shed, for storing firewood.

The horses were all accustomed to her and did not act up. A few nuzzled her, seeking sugar or other treats. "Not today," Evelyn apologized. She paused to pat her pony, then entered the shed. Saddles were lined up in a row on a bench. Bridles and such hung from the walls. The bridle she wanted had been partially split, and placed on a peg on the rear wall. It had not been used in a long time, but the last time it *had* been used was on the sorrel.

Eventually her pa would get around to fixing it. He had so much work to do around their home that a bridle did not rank high on his list. Especially when they had half-a-dozen spares.

Evelyn went back out. Blaze had stopped running in

circles and was licking himself. "Here you go, fella," she said, grinning. "This will help you, I bet." But when she held the bridle to his nose and motioned, the result was not what she expected.

The wolf bent his head and sniffed a while, but did not find where Zach had ridden off.

"Drat. It should work." Evelyn was stumped. It had always worked when she was little. She or Zach would take something the other owned, like a hat or mittens or something. When they held it to the wolf's nose, Blaze knew which one of them he was supposed to track down. And off he would go. As simple as that.

"What's wrong? Have you forgotten the trick we taught you?" Evelyn asked. She tried again.

Blaze sat on his haunches and looked at her expectantly. Maybe, she reasoned, he did not realize what the sorrel's scent had to do with Zach. Or maybe the scent of so many horses hindered him from picking out the sorrel's from all the rest.

Beckoning, Evelyn led him around to the back. Her brother had headed west, along a trail they frequently took to reach that end of the valley. She held the bridle to Blaze's black nose, pointed at the ground, and said, "Fetch him, boy! Fetch Zach!"

Blaze lowered his head and started off.

Evelyn giggled. She had done it! Then the wolf halted and glanced back at her, seemingly confused. "What is it?" Baffled, she scratched her head. She had to think. Her pa had taught her that every problem a person faced could be solved with a little thought and a lot of common sense.

Blaze would not follow the sorrel's scent. So either the scent on the bridle had faded, or the scent on the trail was mixed with that of her father's bay and other horses that had gone up it recently, and the silly wolf still could not pick out the one it was supposed to.

"You can be a pain, you know that?" Evelyn scolded. She stared at the cabin, then at the corral. It wouldn't take long to saddle her pony. She could lead Blaze off a ways, and hope he caught on later. Once he did, that fantastic nose of his would enable him to hunt her brother down in two shakes of an antelope's tail.

She had to hurry, though. Her folks would miss her before too long. She scooted to the gate again. Since she would not be gone more than half an hour, she did not bother to go into the cabin for a parfleche of food. Or a rifle. Her parents were bound to ask what she was up to, and refuse to let her do it.

Evelyn quickly saddled her pony, led it out, closed the gate, and mounted. Blaze was marking a bush. She had always thought it so stupid, the habit wolves and coyotes and the like had of lifting their legs to pee on things. Once she had remarked about how ridiculous it was to her mother.

"That is males for you. They always do strange things."

"Pa is a male and *he* doesn't."

Her mother had snickered. "Daughter, you will find, as you grow older, that all males do things women would never do. I love your father dearly, but he is no different from the rest."

"What does he do that is so strange?"

"I would not know where to start."

"But if men are so weird, why do women marry them? And live with one their whole lives through?"

"Because we are, as your pa would say, gluttons for punishment."

Evelyn never had understood why her mother had laughed so heartily. But she had to admit her ma had a point. The longer she had been around her brother, the more she'd realized how strange males truly were.

At the first bend, Evelyn twisted. Guilt pricked her conscience. It was wrong to sneak off as she was doing, but she told herself it was for a good cause. And she would only be gone a short while. With any luck she would get back, put the pony with the rest, and traipse

119

indoors as merrily as you please, her folks none the wiser.

Blaze padded along at the pony's heels, tongue lolling.

Evelyn had a fair idea of where her brother had gone. Of late, when he went hunting, he was partial to a range west of their valley. To reach it, he had to cross a pass high on a mountain. Since neither her pa nor anyone else had been up that way in a coon's age, the only fresh scent should be the sorrel's.

It was a nice day for a ride. The bright blue sky, the sunshine, the green woods and emerald slopes were too beautiful for words. She trotted on, lost in admiration of the scenery. The antics of some chipmunks made her laugh. A young hawk soaring among the clouds made her wish she could spread her own arms and take wing.

Evelyn had guessed it would take her five minutes to reach the spot she wanted, but it was more like fifteen. The main trail continued on, and would bear to the southwest later. The Utes had used it a lot in the old days, before her pa had claimed the valley for his own. A smaller trial branched off, winding to the northwest, to the pass.

At the junction, Evelyn reined to the right. For another quarter of an hour she rode at a brisk walk. On a switchback that gave her a magnificent view of the entire valley, she stopped and dismounted. The lake shimmered like a gigantic jewel. Tendrils of smoke curled from the cabin's chimney, which she glimpsed among treetops.

Blaze was interested in a marmot burrow. Evelyn called him, wagged the bridle under his nose, and pointed at the base of the slope. ''Fetch Zach, boy. Fetch Zach.''

The wolf tried. He roved the switchback, sniffing every square inch, finally halting where hoofprints led upward. But he did not go up. He stood staring and whining, as if unsure.

''Consarn it all. What is the matter with you?'' Evelyn took a few steps past him and motioned. ''This is the right way! So go! Find that idiot brother of mine! He'll be tickled pink.''

Blaze did not move. He only looked at her and whined some more.

''Are you a wolf or a mouse?'' Evelyn demanded. He was acting scared, which just couldn't be. What did a wolf have to be scared of? She squinted at the pass, a notch in a high cliff wall. It would take her the better part of an hour to reach it. Her folks were bound to realize she was missing, and they would be mad. Her ma, in particular, would see fit to punish her for breaking the rules.

Her pa seldom disciplined her anymore. He might well be the toughest man in the Rockies, but he always treated her as if she were a princess. Even when she did wrong. It had annoyed Zach no end that when they got into trouble for spatting or whatnot, their father was always harder on him. Even when both of them were equally to blame, or she had instigated it.

Zach had complained to their ma. One day her parents had had a long talk. Afterward, her mother had always decided what Evelyn should do to make amends for misbehaving. And her mother was much stricter.

Evelyn gazed at the tendrils of smoke, mulling what to do. She was probably in trouble already. Her pa would have gone out to see what was taking her so long and found the pony missing. He would come after her on his big bay, which could cover ground twice as fast as her animal.

She turned, studying the route to the cliff. Now that she thought about it, she recalled her father had been up this way in the past week or so. Maybe that explained why Blaze was standing there like a bump on a log. If she went to the pass, the wolf should pick up the sorrel's scent with no problem.

''The things I do for my dumb brother,'' Evelyn said aloud as she climbed back into the creaking saddle. ''Let's go, Blaze.''

Up the slope they loped. She was not unduly worried about predators. Her pony might be slower than the bay, but it could still outrace most any other creature. And she had her pistol. And Blaze was there; he would protect her just as he had always done.

They had not gone far when the huge wolf stopped and whined again, louder than ever, as if to get her attention.

Evelyn slowed and gestured. "Come on, you contrary critter! You're the one who's been so all-fired worked up about seeing Zach again. I'm doing you a favor, you know."

Blaze heeded, but slowly, his shaggy head roving over the large boulders that lined both sides of the narrow thread of a trail.

Evelyn clucked to her pony. It went a little farther. Then it, too, slowed. Ears pricked, it nickered. She raised the reins, but as if he were there with her, her father's advice from long ago rang in her ears.

"Always rely on your horse. Horses can hear better than we can. They also have a better sense of smell. So when yours acts up, don't take it for granted it's afraid of its own shadow or a stick. Something else might be to blame. Something a whole lot worse. And the only warning you'll have is your horse."

To her right and left reared scattered boulders half the size of the family's cabin. A jumbled pile on Evelyn's right was the legacy of a rock slide long ago. Usually chipmunks would be scampering all over them, but not today.

"I don't like this," Evelyn declared, her hand straying to the flap of her beaded bag. She should have been more alert. She should have caught on sooner.

Suddenly Blaze growled.

Evelyn glanced at him, then in the direction he was staring. Her breath caught in her throat. From out of nowhere a tawny shape had taken form and substance, a long, sinewy creature with razor-tipped claws and teeth.

A painter, some called it. Cougar, others preferred. She liked the name her pa was partial to.

Mountain lion.

Louisa May Clark awoke slowly. She felt warm and comfortable, for the first time in many days. She was reluctant to wake up too fast. Sluggish in mind and body, she lay quietly, dreamily, half wishing she would fall back to sleep.

She could not quite remember where she was. Her father's grisly death she would never forget. But what had she done afterward? Ah. In a spurt of memory she relived some of it. Her flight. Her fear. The loneliness. Then she had met someone. Who?

A face floated on the insides of her eyelids, a handsome face with a dazzling smile. It was the face of an Indian, or someone who was part Indian, but she was not afraid of him. Nor did she hate him, as she rightfully should. No, she drank in the image of the handsome vision as a parched wanderer would gulp down refreshing water after a trek across a scorched desert.

Stalking Coyote. She remembered his name now, and how she had laid herself down next to him the night before. Shameless hussy! her father would say. Did she have no morals whatsoever?

Smiling, Louisa opened her eyes. And tensed. She was not lying *next* to him. She was lying *on* him! And her head was not on the ground. It was on his chest. A blanket lay over both of them. His arm was around her shoulders. She didn't recall this part, and she wondered what else she had forgotten. How shamelessly *had* she behaved?

His chest rose and fell steadily. He was still asleep, even though the sun was an hour high in a lake-blue sky. Louisa tilted her head to study his wonderful features. In repose they were softer, even more handsome—if that were possible. She had a most unsettling urge to run her fingertips over his lips.

123

What is happening to me? Louisa asked herself. Why was she doing things she never had before? Why was she having thoughts no decent girl ever should? Her parents, were they alive, would cringe in reproach and remorse.

Yet Louisa could not help herself. She marveled at how black his hair was. At how hard his body felt. At how a tiny vein on his neck pulsed to the beat of his heart. Evidently, he had thrown the blanket over them to keep her warm. Or was it for another reason?

For a moment Louisa feared he might have taken liberties. But a glance assured her she had not been violated. Her clothes were intact. Her body felt as it should. Many men would have taken advantage, but Stalking Coyote had not. In her exhausted state she would have been helpless—but he had behaved with honor.

A comment her mother made years ago, one she had forgotten, was recalled with perfect clarity: "When you find a man who will respect you, little one, then you have found the one for you. All men lust. Many men love. But only few ever learn true respect. That is the kind of man you want."

Louisa started to sit up. Instantly, Stalking Coyote's eyes snapped open. His hand dove for a pistol at his waist. Then he saw her, and relaxed.

"About time, sleepyhead," he said.

"Me?" Louisa responded. "I've been awake for ten minutes. You're the one wasting the day away."

Zach could not get over how beautiful she was in the rosy light. "I woke up before daybreak. You were still out to the world, so I didn't disturb you. I figured you had a lot of rest to catch up on."

"How sweet of you," Louisa said.

"I'd have done the same for anyone," Zach said, sure he was blushing. He did not tell her that he had lain quietly for half an hour after he woke up, reveling in the splendor of her features and the feel of her body against his. He had wanted to hold her even closer. To run his hands through her hair. To kiss her. Instead, he'd let himself drift off to sleep again.

"I'll fix breakfast," Louisa proposed. It was the first thing her mother had always done each day.

"I'll get the fire going and tend to the horses," Zach said. Chores his father did every morning. After gathering logs, he arranged them in a circle, the inner ends almost touching—similar to the spokes on a wagon wheel.

Louisa was mystified. "I've never seen anyone make a fire quite like you do," she remarked while chopping rabbit meat into bite-sized bits.

"This is how Indians do it," Zach explained. "It reduces the smoke so enemies cannot spot them."

"Good thing you came along, then," Louisa joked. "My fires gave off enough to gag a buffalo."

"So I noticed. How do you think I found you?"

She giggled. "I'm glad I was doing it wrong if it brought us together."

Awkward minutes elapsed, with neither of them saying a word until they were halfway through breakfast.

Zach liked how she had cooked the meat until it was well done and flavored it with gravy made from elk fat. The combination was tantalizing. "You're a good cook."

"Passable," Louisa amended, pleased beyond measure. Something else her mother had said sprang full blown into her mind. "You'll hear a lot of women say that the way to a man's heart is through his stomach. And you know what, daughter? It's true. Even if a man can cook better than you, he'd rather eat your cooking than anyone else's. Men take it as a token of your love. Just like they do when you mend and clean. But cooking always counts for more."

"Almost as good as my ma," Zach said. As far as he was concerned, his mother was the best cook who had ever lived.

"I can't wait to meet her," Louisa responded, although she was nervous at the prospect, afraid his mother would not approve of their interest in one another.

The next order of business was preparing the elk meat. Zach constructed several racks to dry it on, employing slender limbs and rawhide. "We won't be able to leave until tomorrow," he informed his companion. "Noon, at the earliest."

Louisa could not have been happier. The longer they took, the more time she spent in his company. Just the two of them. They could get to know each other better. Maybe grow closer. She grew all warm and tingly just thinking about it.

By about two in the afternoon the last of the elk meat had been carved into thin slices and hung on the racks. Their time was their own.

Zach was at a loss as to what to talk about. He had never been alone with a girl for so long—not even with his sister. Afraid he would make a fool of himself, he kept his mouth shut.

Louisa did not know what to think of his silence. She blamed herself, suspecting she had accidentally done or said something to offend him. After trying a number of times to draw him out of his shell, without success, she was at her wit's end. Since he did not seem interested in talking, she reckoned it was as good a time as any to treat herself to that bath. "I'm going to the stream," she announced, rising from the log.

"I'll go with you," Zach said. He was eager to do *something* other than sit there like a wart on a toad.

"I don't want to bother you," Louisa said. She did not come right out and say she did not want his company, for fear of angering him. But under no circumstances would she take a bath in his presence!

Snatching his Hawken, Zach declared, "No bother at all. Bloods and Piegans come through this area now and then, and I'd hate for you to fall into their hands."

"You would?"

The radiant smile she bestowed on Zach was bright enough to illuminate the blackest night. "No one should ever be held against their will,'' he said huskily. ''I was a captive once, so I know how it feels.''

Here was a subject ripe for discussion, Louisa mused. ''Who captured you?''

''The Blackfeet.''

''And you're still wearing your hair?''

Zach chuckled while ambling to the north. ''It wasn't as bad as I always feared it would be. They aren't as mean and despicable as most people make out. They treated me decently.''

Louisa was quite surprised. ''My pa always said the Blackfeet, Piegans, and Bloods are the worst of the lot. That they'll as soon kill a white man as look at him.''

''They've hated us ever since the Lewis and Clark expedition,'' Zach disclosed. ''Meriwether Lewis and his men got into a tussle over some guns the Blackfeet were trying to steal, and a Blackfoot warrior was killed. Another was wounded. So they've hated us ever since.''

''That's hardly right. It was their fault. Why is it red men are always so willing to think the worst of whites?''

Just a day ago Zach would have bristled at the statement. Now, he responded, ''I could ask the same about white men. But in this instance you're right. Both sides were to blame. Innocent trappers have been paying with their lives ever since.''

''What would they do to me if they caught me? Kill me?''

''No.'' Zach shunned details. He had suffered enough embarrassment since they met. ''Don't worry, though. I won't let them get their hands on you.''

''My protector,'' Louisa stated with uncommon pride. ''I feel safe with you by my side.''

''You do?'' Zach was flattered, but also practical. Alone, he would not be able to save her should a war party catch them by surprise. The best he could do was put a ball into her head if it appeared they would be taken prisoner. So he was extra vigilant as they approached the stream.

A grassy glade ringed by cottonwoods bordered gurgling water. Dappled by sunlight, a tranquil pool enticed Louisa to its edge. She dipped her hands in, washed them, then drank.

Zach had quenched his own thirst earlier when he brought the horses. Idly scanning stark mountains to the southeast, he waited for her to finish. A bee buzzed past, and he followed its flight to a patch of flowers above a gravel strip that jutted into the stream like an accusing finger. An imprint in the center was cause for concern. He walked over.

Louisa had not been this happy in years. She felt so happy, in fact, she was racked by guilt. Less than a week ago her father had died. Yet here she was cavorting with a young man, a man who was as much a mystery to her as life itself, and entertaining notions no upstanding young lady ever should. She began to wash her face and neck.

Zach hopped off the bank onto the gravel. The imprint was a track, made by an unshod horse. He found several others, less obvious. A rider had forded the stream a couple of days earlier, heading due north. Zach peered into the distance.

"Something wrong?" Louisa asked. Stalking Coyote wore the same look her father had had just before the Indians jumped them.

"We must hurry back and saddle up."

"What?"

"We'll have to leave the elk meat behind," Zach said. He did not like it one bit, not after all the trouble he had gone to. But the packhorses must not be burdened.

Louisa stood. "After all our work? Why?"

Zach could have said, "I do not want any harm to befall you." Or he could have replied, "We must sacrifice the meat to save ourselves." But he did neither. He merely raised his arm and pointed at a long line of warriors descending a tableland. Descending toward the valley, and the stream.

Chapter Ten

The huge cat snarled, a fierce, hissing cry that caused Evelyn King's pony to whinny and shy. Evelyn was so scared, she forgot to firm her grip on the reins. Her mount bounded to the left, brushing against a boulder, and pain seared her leg.

In a lithe leap the mountain lion reached the lip of the high boulder it was on. Crouching to spring, it snarled again, its black-tipped tail twitching.

Evelyn gaped up into savagely piercing eyes, horrible orbs that seemed to stab icy claws deep down inside her. She knew she should wheel her pony and get out of there, but her limbs would not move.

The painter's whole body went rigid. Her pa had told her mountain lions did that when they were about to attack. Evelyn tried to tear her gaze from the cat's, but she couldn't. She sensed that in another second it would be on her, rending and ripping.

That was when a bristling guardian hurtled past. Blaze stood between her and the boulder and growled up at the cougar, which partially rose and cocked its head as if in surprise at the wolf's challenge. The cat's snarls took on a shrill note; its ears flattened. Blaze's hair rose on end, making him appear even bigger than he was, and saliva dripped from his lower jaw.

For long moments the pair glared at one another. Evelyn was sure the cat would pounce. Fear for Blaze spiked through her and broke the spell that held her frozen. She whipped out her pistol, thumbed back the hammer, and fixed a bead on the painter's chest. She tried her best to hold the muzzle steady, but her pony was prancing up a storm. As the big cat stiffened, she squeezed the trigger.

The blast was magnified by the boulders. It sounded as if her father's Hawken had gone off instead of her small flintlock. The ball struck below the mountain lion and ricocheted off, creasing the cougar's foreleg, digging a furrow that oozed red. In a twinkling the painter whirled and was gone, bounding from boulder to boulder in tremendous leaps few living creatures could rival.

Blaze started to give chase, but halted at a shout from Evelyn. The wolf was brave, but foolhardy. It stood no chance against the larger, bulkier, more vicious feline.

Another yell echoed off the slope, from lower down. Evelyn swiveled, then beamed. Galloping toward her was her pa, his whangs flying, his bay lathered with sweat. "Here I am!" she hollered, waving.

Nate King was worried sick. When he had found the pony gone, he had quickly thrown a saddle on his horse and lit out. Winona had wanted to tag along, but one of them had had to stay home in case Evelyn returned. The pony's fresh tracks were as plain as day, and he had pushed the bay to overtake her as rapidly as possible.

Nate had reached the bottom of the slope in time to hear the painter's fearsome cry. Spying the cat, and his daughter, he had barreled up the mountain, seeking a clear shot. Now, watching the mountain lion flee, he gave inward thanks his daughter had been spared. She turned and came to meet him halfway, his relief and her smile

almost enough to make him overlook her willful diso-
bedience. Almost, but not quite. Reining up, he waited
for her to speak.

Evelyn noted her father's stern expression, and knew
she was in for it. When they got back, her mother would
punish her like never before. Until then, she might as
well make the best of the situation. "Hi, Pa," she said
cheerily.

"You were lucky."

"It wasn't so bad."

"That cat would have killed you if Blaze had not been
here."

"It didn't, though," Evelyn stressed to show that all
was well that ended well. "I tried to shoot it, but my
horse wouldn't stand still." She thought to impress him
with how maturely she had handled the crisis, to temper
his anger, in the hope he might convince her mother not
to be too rough on her.

Nate grew sterner. "Do you think I just dropped out
of a tree? I saw the whole thing. You should have shot
sooner." He leaned forward. "What were you trying to
prove? Why did you sneak off?"

"To help Blaze."

"Explain yourself. And it had better be good."

Evelyn detailed how she was only doing her part to
reunite the wolf and Zach. "I wouldn't have gone much
further, honest. Only to the pass. If Blaze didn't pick up
the scent by then, I was going to turn around and head
straight home."

It was something any girl her age might do. But Nate
did not have the leeway parents in the States did. Back
there, when a child misbehaved, it seldom resulted in
injury or death. Here in the wilderness, tragedy was com-
monplace. People paid for their mistakes with their lives.
A cruel state of affairs over which no one had any control. "You should never had left in the first place."

"I was only going to be gone a little while," Evelyn
emphasized.

"You snuck off. You were afraid that if you asked us, we wouldn't let you go. So you broke the rules."

Evelyn was going to deny it, but how could she deny the truth? To lie would only make things worse. "You're right, Pa. But I didn't think any harm would come of it."

"We never do. We think we can do as we please without having to worry about the consequences. That we'll never have to pay for our mistakes because bad things always happen to other people, never to us. Too late, we realize no one ever avoids paying the piper."

Evelyn was not quite sure what all of that meant, but she suspected her father was talking about more than the rules her parents laid down for Zach and her to follow. "What will Ma do to me?"

"That's up to her. I'm giving my own punishment. For the next month, you will do your brother's chores as well as your own."

"Pa!" Evelyn squealed. He had never, ever been so harsh. She blamed the stupid mountain lion. If it had not almost eaten her, her father would not be nearly as angry. "That's not fair!"

"So? Whoever told you life is supposed to be fair? If an unarmed man meets up with a hungry grizzly, is it fair for the bear to eat the man? Is it fair that some people are cripples? Is it fair that liars and cheats can live in the lap of luxury while honest, hardworking folks live in hovels and wear threadbare clothes?"

Evelyn did not see what any of that had to do with her.

"Is it fair that babies are cast aside by their own mothers? Fair that people starve to death in a world of plenty? Fair that people can be murdered in their sleep for the change in their pockets? Fair that you can try and try to get ahead and wind up worse off than when you started?" Nate shook his head. "Life in and of itself is never fair, little one. Get that mistaken notion out of your head here and now."

"I only meant that Zach gets to take it easy at my expense."

"He's had to do some of your chores before."

"Yes, but not all of them. For so long."

"You have to learn a lesson. And sometimes, Daughter, the lessons we learn the best are those which are the hardest."

Evelyn came close to saying, "That's not fair either!" But she held her tongue. She had learned one lesson, at least.

Nate wheeled the bay. "Let's go. Your mother will be worried sick."

"Will it help if I say I'm really sorry?"

"Apologizing is like closing the corral gate after all the horses have strayed off. It's nice to do, but it doesn't bring the horses back."

"What do you mean? I closed the gate before I left."

Sighing, Nate wound down the mountain. He had ridden several hundred yards when it dawned on him that they were shy an animal. He drew rein. "Where did Blaze get to?"

Evelyn looked over a shoulder. She was so mad at having to do her brother's chores that she had lost all track of him. "He was here a bit ago." Fear sprouted. "What if he went after the mountain lion, Pa?"

Nate doubted it. A wolf just wasn't able to bound from boulder to boulder as the lion had done. Rising in the stirrups, he glimpsed a streak of gray high along the trail, making for the gap in the cliff. "There he is. He must be on the sorrel's scent."

Evelyn smiled. Finally! All the trouble she had gone to would not be wasted. Blaze and her brother would be together again. Maybe Zach would be grateful enough to speak to their folks on her behalf, to suggest that she not have to do his chores. Who was she fooling? Zach would never pass up a chance to loaf around doing nothing. She was stuck.

See if she ever did him a favor again!

*   *   *

"I can't see them anymore. How long before they get here?"

"Not long."

Louisa May Clark was running flat out. Minutes earlier the warriors had filed into heavy pines, and now there was no telling where they were. Legs pumping, she was hard pressed to keep up with Stalking Coyote, and wondered if he was holding back for her sake.

Zach willed himself to stay calm. He did not mention that he had seen one of the warriors point toward the stream just before the Indians disappeared in the forest. He came to the clearing, and the sight of the elk meat filled him with resentment. Why should those who had intruded on his happiness fill their bellies at his expense?

"How do you reckon they found us?" she asked. "Did they spot our smoke?"

"No." Zach had taken particular pains to insure they did not give themselves away. "Just dumb luck, I guess."

Louisa crooked her head to see the woods. She tripped over her own feet, and would have fallen if not for Stalking Coyote, who caught her around the waist. "Thanks." She did not mind his nearness. Truth was, she welcomed it.

"Gather everything except the meat while I saddle the horses," Zach directed. There was not a moment to lose. If the warriors had spotted them, men would be sent to both ends of the valley to prevent them from escaping, while the rest spread out and swept the valley floor from side to side.

Louisa did not mind being told what to do. He could throw on a saddle faster than she could. She bundled up the blankets and his parfleche, then untethered the pack-horses and looped the lead rope around the neck of the one she would not be riding. She was ready to go when he gestured for her to climb on.

Out of sheer spite Zach tipped over the drying racks.

He would have burned the meat if there were time, just so the warriors could not get their hands on it. Forking leather, he brought the sorrel to a trot.

"I want to thank you for all you've done for me," Louisa said as they started out. It might be the only opportunity she had, and she did not want to die without showing her gratitude.

Zach absently nodded. He had weightier issues to deal with. What tribe were the warriors from? Were they friendly or hostile? Was it a hunting party or a war party? He hoped they were Crows. While not as partial to white men as the Shoshones, neither were they as bitterly disposed as the Blackfeet. They were wily tricksters who could steal anything right out from under a person's nose. Unless provoked, they rarely slew whites.

Zach stayed to cover as much as was possible. At the ridge, he climbed to within a stone's throw of the crest. The band had done just as he'd figured. Three warriors were to the east, right out in the open. Several others were off to the west, secreted among pines, but one of their mounts moved and gave them away. That left another six who were moving slowly into the valley, strung out at fifty-yard intervals.

Louisa was thankful for the spruce trees that sheltered them. "What will we do?" She whispered, even though the Indians were much too far off to hear her.

"We sit tight," Zach said. Judging by how the warriors were poking into every stand and thicket, it was safe to assume they did not know where he and Louisa had gotten to. For the moment they were safe. But only for the moment.

Zach looked at Louisa. If she was scared, she was putting on a brave front. She did not show it. Here was the kind of girl who would make a fine mate for any man. Brave, dependable, attractive. The very traits his father had said he should look for.

"Something wrong?" Louisa did not understand why he was staring at her so strangely. Not when she was

striving so mightily to please him. If she had done anything she should not have, she must learn what it was
and never do it again.

"You are pretty," he said.

Louisa could have been floored by a feather. Of all the
times for him to choose to compliment her! "I am not,
but it's awful kind of you to fib."

"I am part Shoshone, and Shoshones always speak
with a straight tongue." Zach had more to say, such as
how he took great pride in being known as someone who
always told the truth. But one of the warriors was moving
toward the ridge. "Take a gander," he warned.

Louisa did, and her heart hammered as if fit to explode.
The warrior was one of those who had attacked her pa
and her! It was the same war party! Were they after her?
Or had they stumbled on the valley by chance, as Stalking Coyote believed? "What tribe do they belong to?"

Zach was ashamed to say he didn't know.

"I thought you knew all about Indians," Louisa
teased.

No one knew all there was to know. Not even Zach's
Uncle Shakespeare, one of the most widely traveled
mountain men alive, could make such a claim. Shakespeare had once told him there were scores of tribes that
had had little or no contact at all with the outside world.
Tribes that were more likely than not to view all whites
as potential enemies.

"You have no idea at all?" Louisa would like to know
who her father's slayers were.

"They dress like Piegans, but their hair is different,
more like the Sioux. Yet look at that red circle on the
horse's chest. That's the kind of symbol Flatheads use."

"They must have come here expressly to find us."

Zach was skeptical. The Indians would not have shown
themselves if that were the case. In any event, it was
unimportant. Whether they were from a known or unknown tribe was of no consequence either. Surviving was
all that counted. And to do that, Zach must somehow slip

past them. It was unfortunate the day was so young. Under cover of darkness, sneaking away would be child's play.

Two of the warriors were near the stream, near the pool. One kneed his warhorse into the water and waded to the gravel bar. He bent low, hanging by one arm. Then, rising, he yipped like a coyote, bringing the others at a trot.

"He found where I hopped off the bank," Zach guessed. Soon the warriors would find the clearing amid the saplings. Tracks would lead them to the ridge, and he would have a fight on his hands.

"Should we make a run for it?" she asked.

The idea had merit. Only three warriors blocked the east end of the valley. Better to battle them, Zach reflected, than to go up against six or more. "Stay close. I'll take care of the packhorse."

"No. You'll need your hands free to fight. Leave the packhorse to me."

Their gazes met, and lingered. She was right, of course, so Zach nodded, feeling oddly proud of her. As the Texicans might say, she would do to ride the river with. Grit and wit, grace and charm, all combined in one. That, and she could cook.

"Don't shoot unless I do," he said. "If they spot us, I'll hold them off while you get away."

Louisa dismissed the thought of deserting him with a wave of her hand. "I'm not leaving you."

"It would be best."

"I could never live with myself." Impulsively, Louisa bent and clasped his fingers. They were warm, strong. "I know we hardly know each other, but I care for you. I'm sticking by your side, come what may."

A heavy feeling formed in Zach's chest, like the feeling he had when he suffered from a cold. Only this was stronger, and made him tingle from head to toe as if he were giddy from sipping his uncle's whiskey. "I care for you, too," he heard himself admitting.

Louisa listened to what at first she thought was wind rushing through the trees. But the noise was in her head. She straightened, and was briefly dizzy. What could have caused it?

The six warriors had left the stream and were moving slowly toward the saplings.

Zach wheeled his mount. Enough cover existed to hide them both until they were almost out of the valley. Where it narrowed, the undergrowth thinned. That was when they would be most exposed.

Tugging on the rope, Louisa dogged the sorrel. She sorely missed Fancy. The packhorse did not have as smooth a gait. Worse, it fought the bridle and was uncomfortable with the bit. In a scrape it might act up and put her life in jeopardy.

Zach remembered to favor the shadows, to never silhouette himself against the sky. As a sprout he had spent hours at his father's knee learning woodcraft. Foremost among the many lessons were those on how to keep his scalp when he was in danger of losing it.

"When you're badly outnumbered, run," Nate had instructed him. "Never throw your life away. Never think you have something to prove. There's a fine line between being brave and being stupid."

"But what if I have no choice, Pa?"

"In that case, fight like a wildcat. Or better yet, remember those Vikings we read about in that history book the missionaries swapped me?"

"The Vikings who went mad in battle? The Berserkers?"

His father had nodded. "If you're trapped, go berserk. Do whatever it takes to *live*. Nothing else counts."

"Shucks. Don't worry about me, Pa. I aim to live longer than Uncle Shakespeare."

Aiming to and doing so were two different things. Zach bent low over the sorrel as the tall trees gave way to shoulder-high brush. He held the Hawken down next to his right knee so the metal was less apt to reflect sunlight.

Louisa imitated everything Stalking Coyote did. When he stopped, she stopped. When he continued on, so did she. At any moment she dreaded hearing a war whoop and seeing the entire war party converge.

Presently, Zach reined up. They had about run out of vegetation. Across forty yards of grass were the three men who had corked the bottle, as it were. One had dismounted and was fiddling with his mount's hoof. Another, a stocky man whose face was severely scarred, honed the tip of a lance. The last, the tallest, was fully alert—and armed with a rifle.

Recognition quickened Louisa's pulse. The tall warrior was the one who had let her leave with her pa. She recognized the stocky man, too, as the one who had made such a fuss over it.

Zach twisted. "Keep under cover. If I go down, head east until you see Long's Peak. North of it is a valley about twice as big as this one. In it is a lake, and near the west shore is a cabin. That's where you'll find my folks. Tell them I asked for them to help you."

"What are you planning to do?"

"My ma always said to be polite when I meet strangers," Zach quipped, and without further ado he rode into the open, the Hawken slanted across his saddle.

The warrior examining his horse vaulted astride it. The stocky one leveled his lance and started forward, but stopped at a word from the tall man, who did not move.

Zach did not know which surprised him more, that he was risking his all to save the life of a female he had met less than twenty-four hours before, or that he felt no fear. He had been in bloody scrapes before, and in each, he was ashamed to recall, he had experienced some fright. Why not now?

The tall warrior advanced on a fine dun. Both the scarred man and the third warrior did likewise, both looking as if they would rather fight than palaver.

Thirty feet out, Zach drew rein. He nodded at the tall warrior, who returned the favor. "Savvy English?" When the warrior did not answer, he resorted to Shoshone. "I come in peace. I am your brother, not your enemy." None of them responded.

That left Zach a last recourse. Sign language. His father had begun teaching him "finger talk," as one old trapper had called it, as soon as he was old enough to do the basic gestures. His mother had added to his store of knowledge. So had his Shoshone kin and friends. Shakespeare McNair had rounded out his education by showing him signs McNair had learned during wide-flung travels that stretched from Canada in the north to Mexico in the south, from the muddy Mississippi River to the mighty Pacific Ocean.

Sign language was widely relied on. Tribes that lived on the prairie favored it most, but it was also used by mountain dwellers like the Nez Percé and Utes. Some signs were used by all. Some were more common in the north than the south, or the other way around.

White men who learned it fared better than white men who were too lazy or indifferent to bother. Zach's father claimed it had saved his bacon on many an occasion. Now Zach hoped it would do the same for him. Holding his right hand in front of his neck with the palm out, he extended his index and second fingers straight up. Then he raised his hand until the tips of his fingers were as high as his head. It was the sign for "friend."

The three warriors understood. The stocky man made the sign for, "You lie, boy."

"I fond peace," Zach signed.

"Give me rifle," was the stocky warrior's reply.

The tall man gestured, signing at the stocky man, "I chief. I talk." He did not say "chief" exactly; the sign equivalent meant "elevated," or "one who rises above others." Turning back to Zach, he signed, "I called Tall Bear. Question. You called."

"Stalking Coyote," Zach responded. The leader

seemed reasonable enough. Maybe, just maybe, blood-shed could be avoided. Inwardly, he laughed at himself. A few days before he had wanted to count coup more than anything else in the world. Now here he was—try-ing to avoid counting coup!

The stocky man with the scars snorted. He placed his right hand at the center of his chest, fingers up. Then he moved his hand about a foot to the left, slid it back again, then moved it a foot to the right. It was the sign for "half-breed." The sharpness of his movements reeked of contempt.

Tall Elk glanced at the tall man. He and the stocky man exchanged harsh words in their own tongue, and when they were done, the scarred warrior was quivering with rage. Tall Elk had another question for Zach. "Where you sit."

It was the same as asking where Zach came from. "I sit across mountain," he signed, with a vague motion eastward. Under no circumstances would he reveal more. His parents and sister might pay with their lives.

"Question. White man do."

"I hunt elk."

"Question. You alone."

There was no way around it. Zach answered, "No. My woman with me." Louisa was not truly his, not in the sense that they shared a lodge. But he needed the warriors to realize she meant a great deal to him, to appreciate that he would not part with her without a fight.

Tall Elk's brow creased and he scanned the brush. "Question. Where."

Zach shifted in the saddle. "Come on out, Louisa," he hollered. "But do it real slow, and don't come too far." He smiled encouragement as she complied.

Louisa was as nervous as a mouse in a barn full of cats. She saw the tall warrior's sudden alarm, saw hatred darken the scarred warrior's face. Suddenly it hit her that she had neglected to tell Stalking Coyote she had met these Indians before, that they were the same ones who had killed her father. She prayed she had not made a mistake.

The next moment the stocky warrior hefted his lance, whooped like a banshee, and charged.

Chapter Eleven

On the south shore of the lake was a large log Nate and
Zach had rolled out of the forest the summer before. It
was there because Winona had commented how she liked
to sit and admire the water and the wildlife, and how it
was a shame she did not have anything to sit *on*.

Now, on this bright sunny afternoon, Winona and Evelyn were seated on the log. At opposite ends. Winona
glanced at her daughter several times, noting Blue
Flower's slumped shoulders and exaggerated pout. "Do
you see those baby ducks? They are cute, are they not?"

Evelyn did not look up. She merely said, "Cute." And
went on pouting.

"They are out on the lake, not at your feet."

Against her will, Evelyn lifted her chin a fraction. The
baby ducks were cavorting like kids, chasing one another
and quacking noisily. Ordinarily, it would be enough to
make her smile, but not today. Nothing could make her
smile after the way she had been treated.

Winona folded her hands in her lap and pondered. She

knew how much her pride and joy loved it here, and she had hoped it would snap her daughter out of her funk. But it was not working. "Want to go for a walk all the way around the lake?" Another favorite pastime.

"No, Ma."

"Want to go search for flowers?"

"No."

Winona felt profoundly sad. Her daughter adored flowers more than anything else. "All right. Let us talk about what is bothering you."

"Nothing is bothering me."

Hurt, Winona said softly, "Has it come to this? You would lie to your own mother?"

Evelyn finally looked up. To lie was to go against everything her parents had taught her. Her father said liars were snakes in the grass, the lowest of the low. Her mother had impressed on her that among the Shoshones, lying to someone was the same as striking them a hard blow. "It wasn't an out-and-out lie," she hedged.

"What else would you call it?"

"I'm upset, is all."

"I never would have guessed."

"Please, Ma. I'd rather not talk about it." Evelyn regretted letting her mother persuade her to go for a stroll. She would rather have stayed in the cabin and sulked.

"You would rather go on being miserable and make everyone else miserable besides? That is selfish of you, Blue Flower. I am disappointed."

Evelyn refused to let her mother get to her. "Why should you be miserable? I'm the one who has to do Zach's stupid chores for two whole months."

"Ah. And that has you mad?"

"Darn right it does!" Evelyn had done something she had never done before; she had raised her voice to her own mother. But she could not help herself. It was unfair, what they had done! "It was bad enough Pa told me I had to do them for a month! Then you went and added *another* month! All because I tried to do what I thought was right. I tried to do Stalking Coyote a favor. Now I have to suffer.''

Winona choose her next words carefully. This was an important moment in Blue Flower's life, even if the child did not realize it. A moment on which the girl's whole future depended. A moment every wise parent was on the lookout for, and ready to guide their offspring through. ''So. I was right. You are being selfish.''

''What's selfish about wanting to do someone a good deed?''

''You are thinking only of yourself, not the welfare of our whole family.''

''I was thinking of Zach,'' Evelyn argued. She was bitter, and she did not care. ''Haven't you been listening to a word I've said?''

A cold blanket wrapped around Winona's chest. Never, since the day her lovely child was born, had Blue Flower ever talked to her in such a tone. ''I listen, Daughter. I listen with my ears. I listen with my mind. I listen with my heart.''

''Hearts can't hear.''

''Yours does not, and that is the pity. For if you listened with your heart and not just your ears, you would see why your father and I have done what we have done. You would know we did it for your sake. Because we love you.''

''Punishing someone, Ma, is a mighty peculiar way of showing how much you love them.''

''Is it?'' Winona thought back to when she had been Blue Flower's age, and how she had felt about things. ''Then let us talk about Blaze a moment.''

''I'd rather not. That dumb old wolf is the reason all this happened. I wish he'd never come back. Darn him.''

''He is the reason? Then we should indeed talk about him so I can learn how he is to blame.'' Winona tried not to be too sarcastic. ''Do you recall when Blaze was younger? How much fun you had playing with him, inside and out?''

David Thompson

"Yes, I recollect it," Evelyn said grudgingly. Those had been grand times. Running and wrestling and laughing the days away.

"And do you remember some of the things he did that we did not like?" Winona listed them herself. "How he would wet on the floor? And chew on blankets? And gnaw on your dolls?"

Now *that* Evelyn remembered best of all. One of her best dolls had almost been ruined when Blaze nearly tore off an arm and a leg. "He was too ornery for his own good," Evelyn said.

"A trait animals and people sometimes share." Winona reminded herself to stick to the point. "What did we do to stop Blaze from doing those things?"

"Well, whenever he wet, Pa would rub his nose in it and then kick him outside. When he chewed on the blankets and my dolls, Pa swatted him with a stick."

"We punished him, in other words?"

Evelyn did not like the slant their talk was taking. Her mother could be mighty tricky when she wanted to be. "If you want to put it that way. Yes."

"I do. But it was done for the good of all of us, was it not? So the cabin would not smell of urine. So you and I would not spend hours mending blankets. And so your dolls would not be destroyed."

"You're saying that you punished me today for the good of us all?"

"Let us stick with Blaze for the moment. You agree with what I have said? That we had to do it for all our sakes?"

"I agree," Evelyn reluctantly admitted.

"Did we punish him because we hated him? Do you hate Blaze for what he did to your Flathead doll?"

Evelyn squirmed. "No, I don't—"

"Why did we punish him then?"

"I don't know. Because we liked having him inside with us. And for him to stay inside, he had to learn to behave."

"You're saying we punished him because we loved him enough to want him to be part of our family? That we did it for the good of everyone?"

"Yes, but—" Evelyn saw what her mother was leading up to. "It's not the same as with me. All I did was go off alone. Which I'm not supposed to do, I'll admit. But which would not have hurt anyone but me if something bad had happened."

"Oh?" Winona rested her hands on her knees. "Your father does not love you anymore?"

"What? That's silly. Of course he does."

"And me?"

"You love me, too."

"What about Stalking Coyote? When did he stop caring for you?"

"I reckon Zach does, although he sure has a strange way of showing it sometimes."

"Well, then. Since we love you so much, do you not think we would be deeply hurt if you were to be killed? Do you not think I would cry and cry? That I would go without food and sleep for many days? And want to die myself?"

Evelyn saw tears moisten her mother's eyes, and felt a lump form in her throat. She loved her mother dearly, more than anyone. She could not imagine life without her. "It would break my heart if anything ever happened to you, Ma."

Winona held her arms out, and Evelyn slid along the log to embrace her. They sat quietly, sniffling, for the longest while, until Winona kissed Evelyn on the head and said, "We are a family, precious one. If you are hurt, we all hurt for you. If you were to die, a part of all of us would die." She paused. "We did not punish you to be mean. We did so because we love you, so you will not do what you did ever again. So we need not suffer. We did so for the good of all."

"I'm sorry, Ma. I truly am."

"I know." Winona held her daughter closer, and rejoiced.

"I'll never go off again without asking permission first."

"Thank you."

"I'd never want you or Pa to cry on my account."

"I thank you again."

"Now that I see what you meant, I guess there's no need for me to do all of Zach's chores for two months."

"You guess wrong."

"How about just one month then?"

"How about three?"

"Two is fine."

"Are you sure?"

Mother and daughter drew apart, looked at one another, and laughed. They laughed so loud and so merrily that out on the lake, another mother and her five offspring took startled wing.

It was hard to say who was more surprised by the violent turn of events. Zachary King had given the three warriors no cause to attack. He had bent over backward to be polite, even after the stocky one had insulted him. So when the man suddenly hefted his lance and charged, Zach was dumbfounded. He saw baffled anger etch the countenance of Tall Elk. The tall warrior yelled at the stocky one, who paid no attention.

Louisa May Clark found her voice and cried out, revealing what she should have back on the ridge. "Stalking Coyote! These are the same Indians who killed my pa!"

Zach had only a second to wonder why she had not told him sooner.

The stocky warrior curled an arm to throw the lance. Snapping the Hawken to his shoulder, Zach aimed squarely at the man's chest. He held his fire a moment, hoping against hope that the warrior would heed the tall one and rein up. But the stocky man came straight on, a mask of hate on his swarthy features. The same kind of hatred Zach had beheld in the faces of so many whites. Hatred of him because he was different. Because he was a half-breed.

Zach stroked the trigger.

The warrior had arched his spine and was about to let fly when the lead ball smashed into his sternum and flung him from his warhorse. He crashed onto his head and shoulders, rolled twice, and was still.

The third warrior yipped and charged, notching an arrow to a sinew string.

Zach had not wanted this. He had tried to avoid conflict, for Louisa's sake. Now that it had been forced on him, he did what came naturally. He jerked out a pistol, trained it on the bowman, and fired before the warrior could unleash the shaft.

This time the ball caught its target high in the forehead, blowing the top of the man's head clean off. Momentum carried him onward another dozen feet. He swayed further and further until his legs lost their grip and he tumbled, bouncing to a disjointed stop.

That left Tall Elk. He stared at the stocky warrior, then at the one whose body still convulsed. His face acquired a flinty cast. Uttering a war whoop, he flourished the rifle and jabbed his legs against his mount.

"Please! No!" Zach exclaimed. He did not want to have to kill this one, too. Tall Elk had not wanted to fight. They had no personal grudge, although for all Zach knew, Tall Elk might be the one who had rubbed out Louisa's father.

Zach whipped the second pistol from under his belt and pressed back the hammer. But he did not shoot. Not yet. "Don't!" he hollered, gesturing.

The tall warrior did not slow down. He pressed the stock to his shoulder and tried to hold the rifle steady, all the while thundering closer and closer. He was already so close he could hardly miss.

"Please!" Zach shouted.

Tall Elk's thumb wrapped around the hammer.

"I don't want to hurt you!"

The retort of a pistol was another surprise. For it was not Zach's gun that discharged.

Louisa had drawn one of hers seconds earlier. She did not desire to harm the tall warrior either. But neither would she sit there and let him hurt the one she loved. She fired, and then was jarred. Not by the recoil, by the thought she had just expressed. *The one she loved?* That was impossible! How could she love someone she had only met a day before? She was so shocked, she did not see the tall man fall. When next she looked, he was prone on the ground, trying weakly to raise an arm.

Zach kneed the sorrel to the warrior's side. A neat pink hole in Tall Elk's chest showed he was not long for the world. "I'm sorry," Zach said aloud, sliding the pistol under his belt. In sign he said, "I no fond kill you."

Tall Elk, incredibly, smiled.

Sliding off, Zach knelt. "Great Mystery help your moccasins make track across sky," he signed, then gripped the warrior's hand.

The tall man's smile widened. He squeezed Zach's hand with what little strength he had left. Another instant and his arm sagged, his eyes dimmed. He tried to speak, but no words came out. He exhaled loudly, his eyelids fluttered, and he gave up the ghost.

"Damn."

Louisa hurried up, puzzled as to why Stalking Coyote was so agitated by the death of someone who had been about to slay him. Worried he might be upset with her, she said, "He would have killed you if I didn't shoot when I did."

"I know."

"I didn't want to. I wouldn't be alive if not for him. He stood up for me when the others wanted to do me in." Louisa did not glance at the fruits of her handiwork. She could not bring herself to look at the man's face. Hopping down, she ran to where he had dropped the rifle he had taken from her the day her pa was slain. It was undamaged.

Zach shook himself and stood. "What's done is done." They had a much greater problem. The other warriors would soon be after them. He began reloading the Hawken, advising Louisa to do the same.

"We're up against it, aren't we?" she said. "It's still nine against two."

"We have more guns than they do," Zach said to lessen her concern.

"Who are you trying to fool?" Louisa slid the ramrod from its housing. "My pa told me some bows can shoot as far as guns. And Indians can let fly with their arrows a lot faster than a white person can reload."

Zach did not deny it. His own hands flew as to the west the air was punctuated by harsh cries. He estimated they had five minutes to spare, no more. In half that time he had finished tamping powder and balls into all three of his guns, and was back in the saddle. "Hurry."

Louisa did not bother with her last flintlock. Wrapping the lead rope around her left wrist, she gripped her mount's mane and swung up. "Lead the way, Stalking Coyote. Where you go, I go." She said it lightheartedly, but she meant every word.

Zach sensed as much, and her devotion touched him to his core. "I'm part white, you know," he commented. "I have a white name. Zachary."

"Zachary?" Louisa rolled it on the tip of her tongue, savoring the sound as if it were hard candy. "What's your last name?"

Just then a knot of riders appeared on the crest of the ridge. Zach pointed, wheeled the sorrel, and fled. For the next hour conversation was out of the question. He held the horses to a gallop, only stopping to give them a breather when the sorrel showed signs of flagging.

"Aren't you pushing a little hard?" Louisa asked. Not on her behalf, but for the benefit of the animals. Once, over a year ago, she and her pa had had to outrun some hostiles out on the prairie. As scared as she had been, she would have ridden Fancy into the ground to get away. Her father, though, had set an example by pacing their mounts so neither animal wound up exhausted. The lesson had stuck.

"A little," Zach agreed. But he was doing so for her sake. He would not let the war party get their hands on her.

West of them, tendrils of dust rose above a barren hill.

"They'll never give up, will they?" Louisa asked.

Zach lashed the sorrel and hastened on. He had a plan. Not much of one, but it might work. Two hours later, when he halted again, he shared it. "We have to stay ahead until dark. They're bound to make camp for the night. And while they sleep, we'll push on. By sunrise tomorrow we should be too far ahead for them to ever catch up."

"Should be," Louisa noted. It was risky. By daylight their mounts would be close to collapse, while the war-horses would be refreshed. She commented to that effect.

"Don't fret. There are ways to throw them off the scent," Zach mentioned. "My pa taught me."

By afternoon's end the sorrel and the packhorses were plodding along with heads hung low. But all trace of pursuit had disappeared. At a swiftly flowing stream Zach drew rein and announced, "We'll rest until the sun goes down." Which wouldn't be long.

Louisa ached in places she had never ached before. Her legs were so stiff it pained her to flex them, but flex them she did as she eased her bottom onto a grassy mound and lay back, her head propped in her hands. She could not stop thinking about the tall warrior. He was the first person she had ever slain, and she prayed to God he was the last.

She wondered if the deed had sealed her eternal fate. According to her pa, anyone who broke a single one of the Ten Commandments was not likely to enter the Pearly Gates of Heaven. Was she doomed to Hell then?

Did the Lord hold it against someone when they killed to protect a person they cared for? That couldn't be. Didn't scripture say the Almighty was merciful and just?

Louisa gazed skyward. What else did it say? Wasn't there something about the "Lord giveth and the Lord taketh away"? Her father had been taken from her, and in his place the Lord had given her Zach. Or was she wrong in counting Zach as *hers*? He cared for her. Of that there was no doubt. But how much? How deeply? Was she expecting too much too soon? A shadow fell across her face.

"Mind if I join you?" Zach had stripped off the saddles, then tethered the horses. As tired as the animals were, it was highly doubtful they would stray off, but better safe than sorry.

"Be my guest." Louisa sat up and adjusted her baggy shirt so it fit more snugly.

Zach sat at arm's length. All afternoon he had been mulling over how to say what he had on his mind. Now that the moment had come, he was tongue-tied.

Louisa considered half a dozen things to talk about, and rejected each as childish or silly or both. But there was something she just had to know the answer to. "I never thought to ask. Is there a girl somewhere you're fond of? Back in the States maybe? Or a Shoshone who strikes your fancy?"

Zach laughed nervously. There were a few Shoshone maidens he was fond of. Nothing had come of it, though, mainly because he had not felt the deep stirring in his heart that his pa always said he would when "the right one came along." He'd begun to wonder if it would ever happen. Now it turned out his father had been right. Again. Odd how the older he got, the smarter his father became.

"There is?" Louisa said, not quite knowing what to make of his mirth.

"No. I've never been partial to any girl." Zach had to clear his throat. "Until now."

153

"Oh."

Since she had broached the subject, Zach felt safe in asking, "What are your plans once we're out of this fix?"

"I haven't thought that far ahead. Why?"

Zach fidgeted, then feigned interest in a bug crawling over his moccasin. "You're welcome to stay with us a spell. I'm sure my parents won't mind. Ma always likes to have visitors." He flicked the bug into the grass, annoyed he had not come right out and told her what was really on his mind.

Louisa would like nothing more. But what if his folks did not like her? "I wouldn't want to impose."

"You won't." Zach shifted so he was a little nearer. He liked how her hair curled around her ear, and how small the ear itself was. Dainty, like a tiny flower. "What about you? No fellas you're fond of anywhere?"

She looked right at him. "Just you."

Zach moved nearer still. "It's a mite spooky. I've never felt this way about anyone before. Not even my wolf."

"You have a wolf?"

"His mother was killed in an avalanche, so I took him in." Zach could not take his eyes off her mouth. Her lips reminded him of cherries. Ripe, luscious cherries, like those he had eaten when his family visited St. Louis. He closed his eyes, thinking that when he opened them again her lips would be plain, ordinary lips. But no, they still resembled cherries, and they pulled at him like a magnet pulled at metal. "Would you be powerful upset if I were to kiss you on the mouth?"

Louisa's breath caught in her throat. "You want to kiss *me*?" The only people who ever had were her mother and father, and they always kissed her on the cheek or the forehead.

"If it's okay."

"I suppose it can't hurt," Louisa said nervously. She shut her eyes and puckered as she had seen her ma do many times. Every nerve vibrated like a piano string. She dreaded that she would faint and embarrass herself to no end.

Zach's whole mouth and throat went suddenly dry. He swallowed a few times, but it did not help much. Giving up, he slowly leaned toward her. Fear gripped him. Fear that she would change her mind and slap him for taking liberties. Then their lips made contact, and all else was forgotten. There was just the pressure of his mouth on hers—the slightest of pressure to be sure. Yet it sent a bolt of lightning coursing through him clear down to the tips of his toes.

Louisa was breathless. Her innards felt all warm and squishy. Her heart throbbed wildly. She could feel her skin prickle, as if from a thousand pins. Somewhere, birds were singing. She would have liked for the kiss to last forever, but at length Zach pulled back. "Oh, my," she breathed. "That was nice."

"Nice" did not begin to describe what Zach had felt. He bent to kiss her again, and happened to gaze westward. On a jagged spine of rock riders had materialized, on a spine he and Louisa had crossed half an hour earlier. He shot to his feet and nodded at their determined enemies. "I was wrong. They show no sign of stopping."

The special moment had been spoiled. Louisa would gladly have sold her soul to the Devil if only the earth would open wide and swallow the Indians whole. "But the sun is almost gone. They're going to chase us even after it goes down?"

"So it appears."

"Our horses are tuckered out. They're bound to catch us. What then?"

Zach did not mince words. "We kill them, or we die."

Chapter Twelve

The first packhorse died seven hours later. It snorted and buckled, spilling Louisa, who luckily was unhurt. Ridden to the limit of its endurance, the horse thrashed and nickered, its body lathered with sweat, its mouth rimmed with froth.

Zach had been pushing relentlessly on, refusing to stop even when Louisa pleaded. In the dark he could not see the warriors, but he knew they were back there, knew they were still in vengeful pursuit, knew they would not rest until they had caught up. To save Louisa he would ride all three animals into the ground. But save her he would, or die in the attempt.

As the packhorse spat blood, Zach drew his butcher knife, pressed the blade against its neck, and slashed once, deep. It would hasten the end, lessen its suffering. A shot would be swifter, but the warriors might hear. He guided Louisa by an elbow to the other pack animal, boosted her up, and forked the sorrel. All without saying a word.

Louisa had an urge to cry. She felt so sorry for the poor horse. But now was not the time. Riding at night was hazardous enough without having tears in her eyes.

To say she was bewildered by the change that had come over Zach would be an understatement. Granted, they were newly acquainted. She had just never imagined he could be so grim. So forceful.

As they resumed their flight, Zach was grateful for the full moon. He avoided dense woodland wherever possible. Always, every single minute, he had the Hawken propped against his leg, his fingers on the hammer and the trigger.

Nighttime was made for predators. For the great grizzlies, for roving panthers, for packs of wolves, and more. The mountains resounded to their roars, their snarls, their howls. Often the sounds came from close by. Mingled with them were the bleats and squeals and screeches of hapless prey.

Zach had to always be on his guard. A meat-eater might rush out at them at any given moment. Once, a bear snorted not twenty yards away. Another time, a frightened fawn bounded across his path, appearing so abruptly that he had the Hawken extended and cocked before he recognized what it was.

As if he did not have enough to occupy him, Zach could not stop thinking about Louisa. What *was* he going to do about her? Inviting her to stay with his folks for a while was all well and good, but what about later on? She could not stay with them indefinitely. What were his intentions?

The answer scared him.

Louisa was finding it hard to stay awake. Her eyelids constantly drooped. She would give her head a vigorous shake and sit straighter, but after a while even that failed to help. She yearned to curl up under a warm blanket and sleep until the cows came home, but it was not meant to be. Not yet. Not until they had eluded the war party.

If they did. Louisa was not one of those people who

forever fooled themselves into believing what was not true. She faced whatever life threw at her head-on. The warriors were out for blood, and if they were willing to ride all night long in order to satisfy their bloodlust, then nothing short of death would stop them.

Hour after hour passed at a snail's pace. It was with mixed feelings that Zach viewed the new dawn. Now the predators were less of a threat, but the warriors even more so, for daylight would permit them to ride faster.

The sorrel and the packhorse were glassy-eyed, and the latter kept shaking its head as if it were being annoyed by flies. Only there were no flies. Just as the sun cleared the horizon, it stopped cold, nearly pitching Louisa over its shoulders. She worked the reins and slapped her legs against its heaving sides, but the horse was completely played out. It literally could not take another step.

Zach reined up, dismounted, and walked back. "Get down," he said, sliding out his butcher knife.

This time Louisa could not hold back the tears. "Must you?" she said. "It might recover if we left it in peace."

"You know better."

One stroke and the deed was done. Zach wiped the blade clean on the horse, his gaze on the rugged country to the west. Perhaps a mile off floated a cloud much lower than any other in the sky. A cloud that should not have been there. A cloud of dust. How the warriors had managed to stay on their trail in the gloom of night, he would never know. He had heard of Indians who could do such a thing. Apaches, for example. But he could not, and it amazed him they could.

Stepping into the stirrups, Zach offered his hand to Louisa. "I'm sorry about the horses," he said for her benefit.

"We'll kill this one, too, riding double. He's on his last legs as it is."

"Can't be helped. I'd ride a hundred to death if it meant I could save you."

It was the most wonderful compliment anyone had ever given her. Louisa scrambled up, wrapped her arms around his waist, and kissed the side of his neck.

''What was that for?''

''For you being you.''

Zach had no idea what that was supposed to mean. Who else would he be? He lashed the sorrel to bring it to a trot. A new range rose up before them, the terrain more unforgiving than any so far. Louisa pressed against him, laying her cheek on his shoulder, and for a while he forgot all about the war party and the sad shape the sorrel was in and everything else. The feel of her warm form was indescribably marvelous. It made him tingle all over. Among other things.

More hours were spent scaling switchbacks, crossing divides, winding along canyons. They came to a stream, and Zach forced the sorrel to wade in, then turned upstream and stuck to the middle until the sun was at its zenith. The ploy would delay the warriors, but not thwart them.

Early afternoon. The sorrel plodded up a tree-dotted bench. Zach sagged in the saddle, weary to the bone. Louisa was asleep, her breath fanning his ear, making it hard for him to concentrate.

At the top, Zach reined up. He did not have to search for their pursuers. Half a mile behind were stick figures. Coming steadily on. They never seemed to tire. They never seemed to need to eat. ''They're not human,'' Zach said softly to himself, then gave his head a toss. Enough of that! It was the fatigue talking, not him. They most definitely were human. Flesh and blood, just like he was. As such, they could be stopped. They could be killed.

On to an upland park, Zach goaded his doomed mount. Across it to a rocky saddle, and from there down a steep slope to a meadow so serene that Zach was strongly tempted to stop. Louisa slumbered on, and he did not wake her. She would need to be refreshed later on, when the final clash came.

Zach had never given dying much thought. When it happened, it happened. Violence and death were part and parcel of his life, and had been since he was born. Trappers he knew had been killed by hostiles. Shoshone kin and friends had fallen in battle or been devoured by wild beasts. He had always taken it for granted he would die young, and now he was about to be proven right.

No! Again Zach railed at himself. "Kings are not quitters!" How many times had his pa said that to him? He must not give up. He must resist tooth and nail, as a true Shoshone warrior would. For sweet Louisa. He placed a hand on her arm and gently squeezed. Why did she like him so much? What had he done to deserve her affection? "Many things in life are a mystery, but none more so than love," his Uncle Shakespeare had once said.

Late afternoon now. The sorrel's head hung low, and it stumbled every so often. Zach's chin was on his chest, his eyes half-closed. He willed himself to stay alert, but his body refused to obey. He thought of how short life was, and how precious. Like most, he had always taken it for granted. He vowed that if he lived, he would never do so again. He would live each day to the fullest.

Twilight. The sorrel stopped and would not move, even after Zach whipped it with the reins. Realizing it was pointless, he looked up, and was riven by shock.

For the past half an hour Zach had not been paying much attention to their surroundings. His oversight had cost them dearly, for they had blundered into a narrow, high-walled gorge. Sheer cliffs towered to the right and the left. He looked over his shoulder, and saw the gorge mouth a full quarter of a mile distant.

Ahead, only a few hundred yards, was a bend. Beyond it, quite possibly, was another way out. He tried once more to spur the sorrel forward. Wonder of wonders, his mount stumbled on, and they moved slowly to the stone outcropping. Louisa stirred as they went around it. The hopeful gleam in Zach's eyes faded, smothered by anger that lent life to his sluggish limbs.

"How could I have been so careless!"

The outburst roused Louisa. Blinking, she straightened and stared about her in confusion. "Where are we? Have we lost them?"

"No. I've trapped us."

Louisa saw sheer rock ramparts on either side and a steep talus slope ahead. Talus, that slippery combination of loose earth and small stones. As slick as ice for man and animal alike. "Turn around and go back," she said.

Zach tried, but the sorrel refused. It had given its all, and could give no more. Disgusted more at himself than the horse, he swore and swiftly slid down. "We're on foot from here on out. Let's get out of this gorge while we still can."

His alarm was contagious. Louisa clasped his hand, and they ran back to the bend. She was behind him, so when he suddenly halted, she nearly knocked him down. "Sorry!" she exclaimed, recovering her balance. But Zach was not listening.

Into the mouth of the gorge had filed six warriors. Shadows shrouded them as they spread out from cliff wall to cliff wall, the man in the center motioning as if he were in charge.

"Why are there only six?" Louisa wondered. "Nine were left. What happened to the rest?"

"They took the bodies of Tall Elk and those others we killed back to their village," was Zach's guess. Which was fine by him. The fewer there were, the better their chances. He ran back, pulling her with him. The warriors had not spotted them yet. They had the element of surprise in their favor.

Louisa felt sorry for the sorrel. Its whole frame slumped, its head hung low. It was breathing as loud as a bellows, blood trickling from a nostril. She doubted it would live out the day.

Zach was thinking the same thing. Going over, he quickly removed the saddle and the saddle blanket and placed them near the north wall. The talus slope was like a gigantic, pulverized ramp. Climbing to the top was possible, but it would take forever. Footing would be treacherous, doubly so after dark.

"Come on," Zach said, and started up. Immediately, loose gravel rattled out from under his moccasins. He tried to step only on sizeable stones or flat boulders, which were less likely to slide, but they were few and far between. Using the Hawken as a crutch, he covered ten yards. Twenty.

Louisa had never tried to walk on talus before. She had heard stories, though, about mountaineers who had lost limbs and lives in the attempt. So she was extra wary, lowering each foot lightly, her calves bunched to firm her legs. Imitating Zach, she leaned on her rifle for added support.

Zach was calculating how much time the warriors would need to reach the bend. They would be cautious, anticipating an ambush. So he figured seven to ten minutes. It had to be enough. More stones and dirt clattered down, some spilling against Louisa, who stood stock still until the talus stopped shifting. "Sorry," he said.

"It wasn't your fault," Louisa responded. Talus was like quicksand in some respects. It was as molten as mercury, as unpredictable as a rattler. She eased her left foot up, then her right. So long as she did not rush, so long as she waited a few seconds after setting each leg down, she would be fine.

Or would she? Louisa felt the talus move again. She stayed still, but it did not help. Her feet slid downward as the stones under them flowed toward the bottom, picking up speed as they went.

"Grab this!" Zach declared, thrusting the Hawken's stock at her. She grabbed it and held on, the slope around her rippling like water in an ocean. And like the ocean, it grew calm after a bit.

"Thanks." Louisa pulled herself toward him, but her added weight on the rifle caused his own feet to begin to slide. She promptly let go. "It's hopeless."

"So long as we are alive, there is always hope," Zach said, quoting his mother. An enormous boulder forty feet higher up, and to the right, was his goal. "That's where we'll make our stand."

Louisa thought he must be insane. Pebbles and the like were constantly raining lower. She slipped five or six times, and it was only by the grace of the Almighty that she didn't wind up where she had started with her body battered black and blue. "I hope you know what you're doing."

"I always know," Zach quipped. In this instance he was doing what he felt was best for her, not necessarily for him. Were he alone, he would take the fight to his enemies. But now his priority was her safety. Getting her to cover came before all else.

The rap of a hoof warned Zach how close the warriors were. It was still ten feet to the boulder. Ten feet! Taking a desperate gamble, he said, "Give me your hand."

Louisa deduced what he was going to do. It was madness. A single misstep would reap disaster. "Maybe we should just take our time."

"Maybe you would rather look like a porcupine," Zach rejoined. Entwining his fingers with hers, he grinned, then bounded toward the boulder, taking leaps an antelope would envy.

Her heart in her throat, Louisa did the same. The talus gave way, spewing a torrent of earth and stones. She could not keep her balance for the life of her. Frantically holding onto Zach, tilting first one way and then another, she jumped for all she was worth, jumped again and again. On her third spring a gaping cleft opened, and she started to drop.

Zach yanked, straining every muscle in his shoulder. She came out of the hole so fast, she bumped into him, almost spilling them both. He tottered, the boulder so close, yet not close enough. A cry from the gorge floor heralded the crack of a rifle. A slug missed them by inches and whined off a rock.

Louisa glanced over her shoulder. The six were down there, still mounted. A burly man sent a shaft whizzing toward them. "Look out!" she yelled, throwing herself to the left and wrenching on Zach's arm. The shaft buzzed by, so close she could have reached out and touched it.

More and more talus cascaded out from under them. Zach feared they would be swept to the bottom, hurled at the very feet of their foes. Girding his legs, he shouted, "One more time!" Then he executed a last, long leap.

Louisa was astonished they made it. She landed off balance, falling against Zach, who flung his arms against the huge boulder. Small stones underfoot oozed like grains of sand, but he and Louisa stayed upright, and within moments the shifting ceased.

Louisa clung to Zach anyway, afraid that if she did not, she would be swept away.

Below them, someone yelped. Zach peered past the end of the boulder. Four of the warriors had started up the slope. One was on his belly, being carried back down by a torrent of talus. The others had realized their folly, and were retreating to solid ground. Releasing Louisa, he sighted down the Hawken at the warrior with a rifle. The man caught sight of him just as Zach fired, and sprang aside.

In the confines of the gorge the blast echoed and re-echoed. The ball cored the warrior's torso, high on the shoulder instead of through the heart as Zach had intended. The man crumpled, but the wound was not mortal. Pushing unsteadily erect, he staggered toward the bend.

Zach shoved his rifle at Louisa and took hers. The rest of the band had also decided that a frontal assault would only get them killed. On foot or on horseback, they raced for the shelter of the outcropping. The slowest was a bowman who was tugging on an arrow snagged in a quiver.

Fixing the front bead on the center of the man's back, Zach fired. He had no compunctions about shooting someone who was not facing him. In the heat of battle there were no rules. It was kill or be killed. "It's either them or us," his pa had once said. "So make damn sure it's them."

The warrior's chest exploded outward. Tottering, he slowly spun to the earth, his eyes wide in disbelief.

Zach had seen such looks before. No one ever *expected* to die. They always thought it would be the other fella, not them. A faulty line of reasoning his pa had warned him against. Zach clutched at a pistol, but there was no one to shoot. The other warriors had made it past the bend. Hunkering to reload, Zach remarked, "We're safe enough for the time being."

Louisa knew a lie when she heard one. They were only a third of the way up the slope. Reaching the top was beyond human ability. The only way out, then, was the same way they had come. It was the old proverb all over again, the one about being caught between a rock and a hard place. Only in their case, they were caught between the slippery talus and enraged warriors.

The sun was about gone. In the gorge the darkness deepened rapidly. So much so that, in short order, Zach could not see the outcropping. Neither could the warriors see them. "If you want to get some more sleep, go ahead," he said. "I'll keep watch."

"Sleep?" Louisa repeated. If she didn't know better, she would swear he was jesting. How could anyone sleep on a bed of talus? With hostiles nearby, eager to slit their throats?

Silence claimed the gorge. Total, nerve-numbing silence. It was broken by loud voices, then the pounding of hooves.

"What are they up to?" Louisa asked.

They were doing what Zach would do were the situation reversed. "They're sending a man on around the gorge to see if he can get above us."

"What for? To keep us pinned here until morning so they can pick us off?"

"Why should they bother, when all they have to do is start a slide?" Zach regretted being so forthright when her fingers dug into his wrist.

The mental image of being buried alive by a flood of talus was enough to give Louisa the shakes. To take her mind off it, she occupied herself loading her rifle. And pondering. They had done their best, but it had not been good enough. If this truly was to be her last night on Earth, she wanted it to be special.

Zach was depressed. He had let Louisa down, and she would pay for his failure with her life. Now they would never get to know each other better. He looked at her again, on the sly, admiring her beauty.

Louisa took an eternity to screw up her courage. She sidled next to the boulder, turning so her back was against it. Inadvertently, she set some stones to sliding, but only a few. High atop the gorge the wind was whistling. "I never thought to end my days like this," she said.

"We're not worm food yet."

"The breeze is picking up," she mentioned.

"So it is."

"Without blankets we'll be half froze by morning." She snuggled closer. "Unless we find some way to keep warm."

Zach dutifully draped an arm over her shoulders. He lost all track of time as they sat cheek to cheek, ear to ear. When she turned and her lips molded against his, he responded in kind. This kiss was even more wonderful than the first. He would have loved for it to last all night long, but a sound high overhead intruded.

Louisa had heard it, too. "What was that?"

"A horse."

"The warrior must have found a way up then." Louisa sank into despair. "We're as good as dead."

Hooves clomped. The horse nickered, and was answered by another past the outcropping. Someone laughed. The war party had revenge almost in its grasp.

In frustration Zach smacked the boulder and declared, "I'd give my right leg for a fighting chance."

On bended knee, Louisa cupped her hands and prayed. She was still mad at God for the loss of her pa, but she still believed. As she had done so many times when prospects were bleak, she called on the Almighty for help.

As if on cue, a shriek rent the night. A shriek torn from the throat of the man on the rim. A horrible scream that rose to a soul-rending pitch, then strangled off to a low whimper broken by loud sobs that eventually died.

Zach did not know what to make of it. He tensed when stones and the like began to rattle down from above. Something was descending the talus. "Don't move!" he whispered to Louisa. The racket grew louder. Whatever it was, the creature went by the huge boulder without stopping. Zach could see—*something*—at the limit of his vision. Something on all fours, gliding like a ghost.

The warriors below jabbered excitedly. One of them hollered up to the man on the rim, but there was no answer.

A rumbling growl filled the gorge.

What happened next would live in Zach's memory as long as he did. A shot answered the growl. But it must have missed. Horrendous snarls erupted, so intensely savage that Zach would have sworn a silvertip had ripped into the four men. Confusion reigned. The warriors screeched and bellowed. Horses whinnied and stamped. The whole time, those fierce snarls pealed off the high walls like the raving of a beast mad with rabies. Louisa clutched Zach's arm in fright, and he could not blame her. He heard a lone horse gallop off, heard a wavering wail and the death rattle of a victim.

Then all was still.

"What was that thing?" Louisa asked breathlessly.

Zach did not know. But they were about to find out. Whatever it was, it was now coming toward *them*.

* * *

Evelyn was digging in the dirt with a tool her father used to punch holes in hides and leather when a footstep brought her head up. A calloused hand lowered.

"You're already in enough trouble. I didn't think you wanted to get into more."

"Sorry, Pa. I was going to put it right back." Evelyn placed it in his palm.

Winona was there, too. She had seen their daughter take the swell-end jack from the tack shed, and had informed Nate. Jointly, they had decided enough was enough. Evelyn must be taught a lesson once and for all. Winona was going to take away her dolls for six months.

Suddenly Evelyn pointed. "Say, who are they, Pa?"

Nate gazed to the west. A pair of riders approached, leading another horse. The setting sun framed them with a golden halo. He had to squint to see clearly. "I don't rightly know."

Evelyn was on her feet. "It's Zach! And there's Blaze beside him! But who is that other boy? And why is Zach riding a dun instead of his sorrel?"

Nate had a better question. Why were Zach and the other boy holding hands?

Winona had been staring hard at the second rider, and now divined the truth. Her hands flew to her throat. All thoughts of punishing Evelyn were forgotten.

Caked with dust and grime, Zachary King proudly reined up in front of his parents and puffed out his chest. "Ma, Pa." He got right to the point. "I'd like you to meet Louisa May Clark. The woman who is going to be my wife."

Nate and Winona looked at one another, then at their son, then at the young lady. They were speechless.

But not Evelyn. She giggled and clapped and bounced up and down. "I'm so happy for you!" She paused. "Does this mean you're going to move out?"

WILDERNESS

#24

Mountain Madness

⬅➡

David Thompson

When Nate King comes upon a pair of green would-be trappers from New York, he is only too glad to risk his life to save them from a Piegan war party. It is only after he takes them into his own cabin that he realizes they will repay his kindness...with betrayal. When the backshooters reveal their true colors, Nate knows he is in for a brutal battle—with the lives of his family hanging in the balance.

___4399-8 $3.99 US/$4.99 CAN

Dorchester Publishing Co., Inc.
P.O. Box 6640
Wayne, PA 19087-8640

WILDERNESS
David Thompson

Follow the adventures of mountain man Nate King, as he struggles to survive in America's untamed West.

Wilderness #20: Wolf Pack. Nathaniel King is forever on the lookout for possible dangers, and he is always ready to match death with death. But when a marauding band of killers and thieves kidnaps his wife and children, Nate has finally run into enemies who push his skill and cunning to the limit. And it will only take one wrong move for him to lose his family—and his only reason for living.

_3729-7   **$3.99 US/$4.99 CAN**

Wilderness #21: Black Powder. In the great unsettled Rocky Mountains, a man has to struggle every waking hour to scratch a home from the land. When mountain man Nathaniel King and his family are threatened by a band of bloodthirsty slavers, they face enemies like none they've ever battled. But the sun hasn't risen on the day when the mighty Nate King will let his kin be taken captive without a fight to the death.

_3820-X   **$3.99 US/$4.99 CAN**

Wilderness #22: Trail's End. In the savage Rockies, trouble is always brewing. Strong mountain men like Nate King risk everything to carve a new world from the frontier, and they aren't about to give it up without a fight. But when some friendly Crows ask Nate to help them rescue a missing girl from a band of murderous Lakota, he sets off on a journey that will take him to the end of the trail—and possibly the end of his life.

3849-8   **$3.99 US/$4.99 CAN**

Dorchester Publishing Co., Inc.
P.O. Box 6640
Wayne, PA 19087-8640

Please add $1.75 for shipping and handling for the first book and $.50 for each book thereafter. NY, NYC, and PA residents, please add appropriate sales tax. No cash, stamps, or C.O.D.s. All orders shipped within 6 weeks via postal service book rate. Canadian orders require $2.00 extra postage and must be paid in U.S. dollars through a U.S. banking facility.

Name_____

Address_____

City_____ State_____ Zip_____

I have enclosed $_____ in payment for the checked book(s).

Payment <u>must</u> accompany all orders. ❑ Please send a free catalog.

WILDERNESS

VENGEANCE TRAIL
DEATH HUNT

The epic struggle for survival in America's untamed West.

Vengeance Trail. When Nate and his mentor, Shakespeare McNair, make enemies of two Flathead Indians, their survival skills are tested as never before.

And in the same action-packed volume....

Death Hunt. Upon the birth of their first child, Nathaniel King and his wife are overjoyed. But their delight turns to terror when Nate accompanies the men of Winona's tribe on a deadly buffalo hunt. If King doesn't return, his family is sure to perish.

___4297-5 $4.99 US/$5.99 CAN

Dorchester Publishing Co., Inc.
P.O. Box 6640
Wayne, PA 19087-8640

Please add $1.75 for shipping and handling for the first book and $.50 for each book thereafter. NY, NYC, and PA residents, please add appropriate sales tax. No cash, stamps, or C.O.D.s. All orders shipped within 6 weeks via postal service book rate. Canadian orders require $2.00 extra postage and must be paid in U.S. dollars through a U.S. banking facility.

Name_____
Address_____
City_____State_____Zip_____
I have enclosed $_____ in payment for the checked book(s).
Payment <u>must</u> accompany all orders. ☐ Please send a free catalog.

WILDERNESS DOUBLE EDITION

SAVE $$$!

Savage Rendezvous by David Thompson. In 1828, the Rocky Mountains are an immense, unsettled region through which few white men dare travel. Only courageous mountain men like Nathaniel King are willing to risk the unknown dangers for the freedom the wilderness offers. But while attending a rendezvous of trappers and fur traders, King's freedom is threatened when he is accused of murdering several men for their money. With the help of his friend Shakespeare McNair, Nate has to prove his innocence. For he has not cast off the fetters of society to spend the rest of his life behind bars.

And in the same action-packed volume...

Blood Fury by David Thompson. On a hunting trip, young Nathaniel King stumbles onto a disgraced Crow Indian. Attempting to regain his honor, Sitting Bear places himself and his family in great peril, for a war party of hostile Utes threatens to kill them all. When the savages wound Sitting Bear and kidnap his wife and daughter, Nathaniel has to rescue them or watch them perish. But despite his skill in tricking unfriendly Indians, King may have met an enemy he cannot outsmart.

__4208-8 $4.99 US/$5.99 CAN

Dorchester Publishing Co., Inc.
P.O. Box 6640
Wayne, PA 19087-8640

Please add $1.75 for shipping and handling for the first book and $.50 for each book thereafter. NY, NYC, and PA residents, please add appropriate sales tax. No cash, stamps, or C.O.D.s. All orders shipped within 6 weeks via postal service book rate. Canadian orders require $2.00 extra postage and must be paid in U.S. dollars through a U.S. banking facility.

Name_____
Address_____
City_____ State_____ Zip_____
I have enclosed $_____ in payment for the checked book(s).
Payment <u>must</u> accompany all orders. ☐ Please send a free catalog.